* * * * * * *

Lora stood in shock at the sight in front of her. Jeff's secretary was trying to retrieve her blouse from the floor at the end of the coffee table. At the same time, Jeff was trying to put some distance between himself and his secretary, but tripped over the woman's long legs and fell in between the sofa and the coffee table.

"Lora!" Jeff finally managed to say as he looked up at her.

The sudden sound of Jeff's voice shook Lora out of her stupor.

"How could you?" she asked, her voice almost unable to get the words out.

As the shock of what she had seen began to wear off, all Lora could think about was getting out of there as quickly as possible. She dropped the bottle of wine and the bouquet of flowers on the floor, turned and ran out of the office. She ran down the hall as fast as she could in high heels, never once looking back.

* * * * * * *

Other titles by J.E. Terrall in
    LARGE PRINT EDITIONS

Western Short Stories
    The Old West
    The Frontier
    Untamed Land
    Tales From The Territory
    Frontier Justice

Western Novels
    The Story of Joshua Higgins
    Conflict in Elkhorn Valley
    The Valley Ranch War

Romance Novels
    Sing For Me
    Return to Me
    Forever Yours

Mystery/Suspense/Thriller
    I Can See Clearly
    The Return Home
    Murder in the Backcountry

FOREVER YOURS

by
J.E. Terrall

ISBN: 978-0-9997823-2-3

Printed in the United States of America
First Printing / 2009   www.lulu.com
Second Printing / 2015   www.createspace.com
Third Printing / 2018   www.createspace.com
Cover: Cover photo taken by author,
J.E. Terrall

Book layout/
Formatting: J.E. Terrall
                    Custer, South Dakota

FOREVER YOURS

To Mike and Kendra Luze

CHAPTER ONE

Lora Winters was a slim young woman with long dark brown hair and dark brown eyes that sparkled when she was excited. On this particular evening, Lora had every reason to feel especially light and jubilant. She bubbled with excitement at the prospect of seeing her boyfriend, Jeff Bowman.

She had spent a good deal of the day planning to surprise Jeff with the news that she would accept his proposal of marriage. Lora had deliberately delayed answering his proposal of marriage until tonight because today was the six-month anniversary of the day they met.

When Jeff had told her that he had to work late on a very important brief for his boss, she had been disappointed but she quickly forgave him. Lora understood that it was hard being the newest attorney in a big law firm, even if his father was one of the major partners. Jeff had suggested they celebrate tomorrow night with a quiet dinner for two, but she still wanted this day to be special.

Lora was convinced that a brief interruption from his work would not be a problem for him. She would not stay more than a few minutes. Just long enough for her to tell him that she would marry him, and for them to have a toast to their future together. They could celebrate their engagement with their friends and family at a later date.

After her shower, Lora walked into her bedroom. She fixed her hair the way he liked it and dabbed on a few drops of his favorite perfume. She carefully selected a short black dress with thin shoulder straps. The form fitting dress clung to her shapely body and accented the smooth flowing curved lines of her form. It was slightly revealing, but that was what she wanted tonight. Since it was a cool and rainy evening, she slipped into a light coat before leaving.

On her way to Jeff's office, Lora stopped at a local floral shop for a small bouquet of daisies, the same kind of flowers he had given her on their first date. Her next stop was at a liquor store for a bottle of their favorite wine.

She drove into the basement garage of the downtown office building where he worked.

Parking her car in the garage, Lora took the elevator to the sixteenth floor. The ride up had her smiling and humming to herself. She was almost giddy with excitement.

As she walked along the hall, she had a lively spring in her step. Lora could hardly wait to see the expression on Jeff's face when he saw her all dressed up. The clicking of her high spiked heels on the polished marble floor echoed in the empty hallway, each step taking her closer to Jeff's office.

As Lora approached the door to Jeff's office, she could hear voices. She was a little puzzled as it had been her understanding that Jeff would be working alone, but it didn't sound like he was alone.

Reaching for the doorknob, she turned it and opened the door to his office. Entering, Lora froze in shock. She could not believe her eyes.

She found Jeff on the sofa with his secretary. He had his arms wrapped around the pretty blond. His shirt and tie had been casually tossed onto the coffee table. His secretary's blouse and bra were lying in a pile on the floor next to the sofa, and her skirt was hiked up almost to her waist. Jeff was lying half over her, kissing her lustfully as he fondled her bare breasts. The woman had her arms around Jeff's neck and was moaning softly as Jeff caressed her breasts and kissed her passionately.

It slowly began to register in Jeff's mind that someone had opened the door. He raised his head and looked over his shoulder. His eyes grew large when he saw Lora standing in the doorway with a shocked look on her face. His jaw dropped at the surprise of seeing her. Jeff was unable to speak or even move. His mind was working overtime in an effort to say something, anything that would make sense.

Jeff suddenly let go of his secretary and pushed her away. He stumbled as he tried to stand up, falling back on top of her. All the time his secretary was trying to get out from under him.

Lora stood in shock at the sight in front of her. Jeff's secretary was trying to retrieve her blouse from the floor at the end of the coffee table. At the same time, Jeff was trying to put some distance between himself and his secretary. Instead, he tripped over the woman's long legs and fell in between the sofa and the coffee table.

"Lora!" Jeff finally managed to say as he looked up at her.

The sudden sound of Jeff's voice shook Lora out of her stupor.

"How could you?" she asked, her voice almost unable to get the words out.

As the shock of what she had seen began to wear off, all Lora could think about was getting out of there as quickly as possible. She dropped the bottle of wine and the bouquet of flowers on the floor, turned and ran out of the office. She ran down the hall as fast as she could in high heels, never once looking back.

When she came to the elevator at the end of the hall, she could see by the number it was still on the sixteenth floor. She pushed the button to open the doors, but it seemed to take forever for the elevator doors to respond. She pushed it again and again until the doors finally opened letting her in.

Once in the elevator, she turned around in time to see Jeff come running out of his office. He was trying to pull his shirt on as he ran down the hall toward her.

"Lora, wait," he called out to her.

She pushed the button that would take the elevator down to the garage level. When the elevator doors didn't instantly close, she pushed the button again and again in a frantic attempt to get the doors to close before Jeff could catch up to her.

As the elevator doors finally began to close, she could hear Jeff calling to her from down the hall.

"Lora, wait. I can ex...," the sound of his voice quickly fading away as the elevator doors shut.

When the elevator began to slowly descend, Lora turned into the corner, covered her face with her hands and began to cry. By the time the elevator reached the parking garage level, Lora's eyes were so filled with tears she could hardly see. She ran blindly out into the garage.

Lora fumbled around in her purse for the keys to her car, at last finding them. She desperately tried to unlock the car door, but tears continued to blur her vision. She finally managed to get the key in the lock and unlocked the door. She jerked it open and got in, slamming the door shut behind her.

She immediately slumped over the steering wheel and began to cry uncontrollably. It took her several minutes before she regained enough control of herself that she could drive.

Lora again wiped the tears from her eyes then started the car. As she backed out of the parking space, she could see Jeff in her rearview mirror. He was just coming out of the elevator.

She watched him for a moment as he stopped and looked around for her. His hair was a mess and his shirt was only half tucked into his pants. Even with tears in her eyes she could see he had put his shirt on in such a hurry that it was not buttoned straight.

She suddenly realized he had spotted her car and was running toward her. Lora quickly stepped on the gas pedal and drove away as fast as possible. She drove out of the garage without looking, almost hitting another car as she turned out onto the street. She raced away from the building without looking back. It took a few minutes for her to understand she was going too fast. She let up on the gas pedal allowing the car to slow down.

As she headed away from the building, she found it impossible to get the picture of Jeff and his secretary out of her mind. Tears continued to run down her cheeks. The feelings of hurt, anger, disgust, and the feeling of being used were beginning to overwhelm her, so much so she had to pull over along the highway and stop the car. Once the car was stopped, she rested her head against her hands on the top of the steering wheel and let herself bawl.

After several minutes of sitting alongside the highway, Lora began to think about what she should do. Lora decided she should not return to her town house. There was no doubt in her mind that Jeff would try to go there to see her. The last thing she wanted was to have to deal with him tonight. She needed time to think, time to put things in perspective, and time to get her thoughts in order. She needed time to make decisions.

At the moment, all she could think about was that Jeff was cheating on her and had probably been cheating on her all the time they had been dating. She was having a tough time trying to understand what she had done to make him seek love and affection in the arms of another woman. What did that woman have to offer him that she couldn't?

As soon as she was able to gather her thoughts enough to make some sense of them, she began looking around. The evening was unusually cold and damp. It had been raining most of the day and into the night. In fact, it had been raining off and on for the past several days.

It took Lora a couple of minutes to figure out where she was parked. She looked around and discovered she was parked on the shoulder of Interstate 70. She had been driving west toward the mountains. Lora had started out not knowing where she was going. She still had no idea where she would go so she would not have to see or talk to Jeff.

Her attention was quickly drawn to the flashing red and blue lights in her rearview mirror. It took a second or two for it to register what she was seeing. A Highway Patrolman had pulled up behind her.

Lora let out a sigh of hopelessness as she rolled down her side window. She wondered what else could possibly go wrong tonight as she watched the patrolman walk up along side the car. She looked up at him as he looked in the car.

"Are you all right, Ma'am?" the officer asked politely, obviously seeing that she had been crying.

"Yes," she replied, her voice chocking a little.

"Are you sure?"

"Yes, officer, I'm fine," she replied, but she didn't mean it or feel fine.

"Do you know you are not allowed to park on the interstate except in an emergency?"

"Yes. I just needed a minute to get my directions."

"Where are you going?"

"I'm going to my place in the foothills," she replied without thinking.

"It's a pretty nasty night. Drive carefully," he said as he reached up and touch the brim of his hat.

"Thank you," she replied as he turned around to leave.

Lora watched him in her mirror as he walked back to his car. She was glad he had not pressed her for the reason she had been crying. She didn't know if she could explain why to him without completely breaking down again.

She had told the officer she was going to the foothills. Now that she had had a couple of minutes to think about it, it didn't seem like a bad idea. Her grandfather's small ranch would be a good place to go, at least for tonight. The phone was not hooked up and she didn't think that Jeff knew about her grandfather's ranch. She had been saving it for a surprise. It would give her a quiet place to think and to take time to decide what she was going to do.

As she pulled back out onto the Interstate, she noticed the Patrolman following her. He stayed behind her for a couple of miles before he pulled off on one of the exits. It was obvious he wanted to make sure she could handle her car.

She drove along Interstate 70 up into the foothills west of Denver. Once in the mountains, she turned onto a narrow winding road that would take her to the small mountain ranch left to her by her grandfather a couple of months ago. It had been a long time since she had been there, but tonight she desperately needed a place where she could be alone. She needed a place where she would not have to deal with anyone.

The headlights of her small car did little to light the way along the dark, deserted road. The night was black and the rain streaked windshield was making it hard for Lora to see where she was going.

As she came around a sharp curve on the mountain road, a deer suddenly darted out in front of her car. Lora swerved to miss the startled animal. The car went out of control on the wet pavement and started to skid. She hit the brakes in an effort to get the car to stop, but the road was too slippery.

She gripped the steering wheel tightly as her car skidded closer and closer to the edge of the road. Lora was frozen in terror as she watched the front of the car slip over the edge of the embankment.

Everything seemed to move in slow motion for her. The car began to slowly roll over and over and over as it went down the steep embankment. She could hear someone scream. It did not even register in her mind that it was her own screams she was hearing. Then suddenly everything went blank.

Lora Winters' car rolled and bounced and tumbled on down the steep side of the deep canyon before it finally came to rest on a narrow ledge on the canyon wall. The car hung precariously over the edge as if waiting for something to cause it to fall deeper into the canyon. The once shiny small car was now nothing more than a mangled hunk of sheet metal, broken plastic and shattered glass.

Lora was pinned in her seat by the seat belt and shoulder strap. It held her tightly against the seat while the deflated air bag hung limp from the center of the steering wheel. It was only the strength of the seat belt Lora had secured tightly out of habit that had kept her from being thrown out of the car and down into the canyon.

Gradually, Lora began to regain consciousness. She slowly opened her eyes only to find it very dark. There were no stars in the sky. There was only a hint of the lights from the city miles away casting a faint glow against the clouds. In the darkness it was impossible for her to even see the dashboard.

Lora felt cold and alone. It seemed to her that she was sitting in a chair, but the seat was leaning sharply to one side. Severely shaken and her mind still clouded from the bouncing around of the accident, she was unable to comprehend where she was or what had happened. Her head begin to clear and rational thought began to creep back into her consciousness.

As her senses returned, her head began to hurt along with other parts of her body. Even with the pain in her head, she began to remember bits and pieces of what had happened. Logic told her that if she could see, she might be able to assess her situation.

She reached for the switch for the headlights, but quickly discovered the lights were already on, but not working. Frantically, she twisted the knob in the hope that the dome light would work only to find it wouldn't come on.

Panic began to swell up inside her and grip her whole being. Her heart began to race and her breathing became rapid and shallow as the hopelessness of her situation slowly sank into her consciousness. She screamed.

"HELP! HELP!"

She waited and listened for what seemed like an eternity for a reply. When she didn't hear anything, she screamed again and again. There was still no answer. A deep seated feeling of being abandoned washed over her. It was highlighted by the realization that no one was coming to help her.

It became clear she was on her own, and it was unlikely help would come any time soon, if at all. If she was going to survive the night, she was going to have to do it without anyone's help.

Lora took in a deep breath in an effort to pull herself together. As soon as she had regained some control of her emotions and was able to think more clearly, she reached out in front of her. Lora could feel the steering wheel of the car even though she could not see it in the darkness. The feel of the limp air bag gave her only a hint of how serious her situation really was.

Reaching past the steering wheel, Lora moved her hand along the dash in an effort to find the glove box in the hope of retrieving the flashlight. Just as she found the latch to the glove box, she remembered she had taken the flashlight out of the car and had failed to put it back.

Already resigned to the fact she could not stay there, she reached for the door handle expecting to find it. It was gone as well as the entire door. There was nothing but a large opening into the vast darkness where the door had been.

Suddenly, there was a flash of lightening followed by the crash of thunder so loud it seemed to shake her entire world. It startled her and made her gasp for a breath of air. Yet, in that split second of light she was able to catch a glimpse of her predicament.

She felt her chest tighten as fear clutched at her rib cage and squeezed it like a vice. Her heart seemed to be racing as well. That brief flash of light had shown enough for her to begin to comprehend her situation. Although it took a moment for it to sink in, she was able to understand that her car was dangling precariously on the side of the canyon.

Another flash of lightening and crash of thunder startled her again. This time she was sure she felt the car shake and even move slightly. Something deep down in the recesses of Lora's mind told her that she had to get out of the car before it broke away from the ledge and fell further down into the canyon taking her with it.

Afraid to move for fear the car would come loose from the canyon wall, she forced herself to slowly slide her hands over the seat belt. Sliding one hand along the shoulder strap, she found the latch.

Since the tension on the belt was tight, she was afraid to unhook the belt for fear it would cause the car to roll on over the edge. She also knew that if she didn't unhook it, she would not be able to get out of the car.

Holding onto the seat tightly with one hand, she unhooked the seat belt with the other. When the seat belt came loose, the car creaked and moaned as if it was in pain then moved slightly. In a state of near hysteria, Lora leaned out of the car and grabbed at anything she could reach.

At first she found nothing to hang onto, but she continued to grope for something, anything she could grab and hold on. Her fingers finally found what felt like the stump of a small tree in the darkness. She grabbed hold of it for dear life and started to pull herself out of the car.

Lora could hear the car groan and scrape against the rocky ledge. She could feel the car slowly begin to move. Clutching the stump of the tree with both hands, and holding on as tight as she could, she pulled herself free of the car. Just as her feet slid out of the car, she heard the ripping, snapping and popping of metal that was bending and tearing as the car started to slide off the ledge. Suddenly the silence of the night was filled with the sounds of her car rolling and tumbling as it went crashing on down the steep canyon wall. It smashed against rocks, boulders and trees as it fell.

Silence once again filled the air when the car finally came to rest on the canyon floor. The only sounds were of Lora gasping for breath and the pounding of her heart as she clung to the tree stump. It frightened her to think about how close she had come to ending up in the bottom of the canyon.

Gradually, she was able to catch her breath and regain some semblance of control of herself. Her fears did not subside, but she was able to gain a small degree of rational thought.

Gradually the rush of adrenalin began to slow and Lora's body began to let her know the extent of her injuries. She could feel the pain on the side of her head, but she could also feel a growing pain in her right ankle and left wrist. She could not tell the extent of her injuries, but she could certainly feel the pain.

Lora had lost all track of time. She had no idea how long it had been from the time she went off the road to when she opened her eyes. The one thing she did seem to understand was she could not stay clinging to a tree stump on the canyon wall. If she didn't do something soon, she might not survive the night.

It was only the basic human instinct to survive that gave her the determination to live. She looked up the side of the canyon, but could not see anything but darkness. It was still raining, although it had let up some. The darkness of the night had completely surrounded her, filling her with the feeling of loneliness and despair.

Slowly, and painfully, Lora pulled herself up. She found a boulder big enough to sit on.

She sat on it while she tried to catch her breath. As she sat there gathering strength and waiting for the pain to subside, she began to realize how much the cold, wet weather had penetrated her entire being. She could not remember a time in her life when she had felt so cold.

Suddenly, there was another flash of lightening followed by the crash of thunder. That split second of light gave Lora a chance to see how precarious her position was. Her chest constricted with fear as she saw nothing below her except a large black hole that appeared to be a bottomless pit. What she did discover was that she was sitting on the edge of a narrow ledge, not a boulder at all. She pressed back against the side of the canyon wall as she tried to get back as far from the edge as possible. Her breath came in short, shallow gasps.

Lora clung to the rocky ledge as she tried desperately to escape the terror that had griped her so tightly. She tried hard to regain control of her thoughts, but it was not easy. Lora closed her eyes and took a few deep breaths in the hope of clearing her head.

"Get hold of yourself. Think," she said out loud.

The sound of her own voice seemed to help her think about what she needed to do. The thought ran through her mind that she would not be missed until at least Monday when she didn't show up for work. By the time anyone would miss her, it might be too late. The only plans she had for the entire weekend had been with Jeff. She knew he would not be looking for her on the side of a canyon, no one would.

Lora realized she would have to find a way out of the canyon on her own. She would have to find a way to get back up on the road where she might find someone to help her.

Determined that she was not going to die on the rocky ledge, she slowly reached out and groped in the darkness for something to hang on to. She discovered a branch or limb jutting out of the rocks. She pulled on it to make certain it was strong enough to bare her weight. It seemed to be solid. Carefully, she wrapped the fingers of both hands around the limb and began pulling herself up. As she pulled, a jabbing pain shot through her left wrist. She cried out, but managed to hang onto the limb.

She tried to get her feet under her so she could stand, but the pain in her right ankle shot through her entire body causing her to cry out again. With nothing but shear determination, a lot of effort and tolerating a great deal of pain, she managed to stand up on the ledge. Hanging onto the limb with her uninjured hand while standing on one leg, she rested for a moment while she waited for the pain to diminish and to catch her breath. Her only hope of getting out of the canyon was to crawl, but even that would be difficult given the steepness of the canyon wall and the extent of her injuries.

After taking a moment to rest and gather her strength, she let go of the limb. She reached out and felt the rocks and ground around her. Climbing up would be difficult enough if she could see, but almost impossible since it was too dark for her to see anything that was not within easy reach.

She let out a long slow breath as she tried to suppress another wave of hysteria that was starting to wash over her. In a stubborn effort not to let it overwhelm her, she mashed her teeth together and silently refused to give in to it.

"This is no time to panic," she told herself.

Her life depended on her being able to keep herself in control. It was time for her to find out just how strong a woman she really was.

Reaching out in front of her again, she painstakingly inched her way up the side of the canyon wall. She crawled from one rock to the next, from one limb or branch to the next, each time dragging herself a little further up the canyon wall. She had to stop every few minutes to catch her breath and to give the pain in her body a chance to lessen before she pressed on.

In the darkness she was able to shut the rest of her world out of her mind and concentrate on getting up the canyon wall. It seemed like it had taken her hours to move only a few feet.

A sense of exhilaration gripped her as she pulled herself up over the edge of a ledge and onto what appeared to be a level flat area. The only thing she could think of that might be level was the road she had been driving on.

Believing she had finally made it back to the road, she could hardly contain her excitement. Her heart raced and a sense of renewed hope raced through her body as she pulled herself up onto the level ground.

After a few minutes of rest, Lora began crawling around on her hands and knees in an attempt to find the edge of the road. While feeling the ground looking for the pavement, she thanked God for helping her. She was absolutely certain she had found the road.

There was another flash of lightening that lit up the area for a brief second giving her a chance to see the ground in front of her. As the darkness once again wrapped itself around her, she began to realize there was no pavement. The road she had been expecting to find was not there. The ledge went in both directions, but it was not a road. There was no way for her to know where it went, or if it went anywhere at all.

Panic once again began to grip her and caused her chest to constrict. The hopes she had of surviving the ordeal rapidly escaped from her. It was beginning to be replaced by a sense of loss and a feeling of despair.

She was wet and cold, and her head was throbbing. Her wrist and ankle were burning with pain. The only thing she was sure of was the ledge was not the road to her ranch house. She had no idea where she was, but she was convinced she was a long way from her destination. She began to think that it didn't make that much difference how far she had to go for help. At this point, any distance was too far for her to go in her condition.

Lora began to realize she was not only injured and exhausted, but she was now lost. She could hear the sound of thunder off in the distance and see the lightening in the distant clouds, but there was little light to help her see what was more than a few yards around her.

She looked both ways, up and down the narrow ledge, but she couldn't see anything. Even if she could see, she had no idea which way she should go to find help. Even if she knew, she was convinced her swollen and painful ankle would not allow her to walk.

The sounds of the rain falling into small pools of water, and the sound of the thunder off in the distance as the storm moved further away, did nothing to raise her spirits. Her feelings of hopelessness overshadowed any possible thought that she might be found.

Resigning herself to her situation, she crawled over to a small tree. She sat on the wet grass and leaned back against the tree as she looked out into the darkness and began to cry. Her tears mixed with the rain as it ran down her face. She was soaking wet and the cold was beginning to penetrate to the bone.

Time passed slowly before the rain finally turned into a slow steady drizzle, but Lora didn't even notice. She lay over on her side and curled up in a fetal position at the base of a small tree in an effort to try to stay as warm and dry as possible. She could not keep her body from shaking or her teeth from chattering.

Lora knew that if she went to sleep she might die, but she couldn't help herself. She was too weak and too tired to resist the desire for sleep. She closed her eyes and let sleep come in the hope it would relieve some of her pain.

CHAPTER TWO

There had been some thunderstorms with heavy rains at times over the past couple of days, but last night seemed to have been the worst. Mark Howard had gone to bed early since the power to his ranch house had been out since yesterday evening. Power outages were fairly common in the foothills west of Denver, especially during late afternoon and early evening spring storms.

Mark's dog, Casey, had awakened him with a need to go outside. Mark rolled over and looked at the clock. It was four-thirty in the morning. Reluctantly, he got up and lit a lamp. He dressed in jeans, a sweatshirt and boots.

Mark walked through the kitchen to the back door and opened it for Casey. Once Casey was outside, he looked out. It was still drizzling and the air was cool. As soon as he let Casey out, he checked to see if the power was back on and if the phone was working. They were not.

Mark returned to the kitchen to fix himself a cup of coffee on the gas range. While filling the pot with water, he began to think about the drive from the road to the ranch house. After several days of rain there was a good possibility the drive might wash out in a couple of places. If that occurred, he would not be able to get out until he fixed them. He became concerned about the drive.

Mark had built his ranch house in this out-of-the-way place for the sole purpose of getting away from the city and its people. Being isolated from the rest of the world was fine with him. Besides, he was close enough to Denver he could go to the city anytime he wanted.

As far as his work for the newspaper was concerned, he could still write his weekly column at the ranch house. With all the conveniences of computers, phones and fax machines, he could do most of his work in the mountains, unless the power went out.

Living in the foothills gave him inspiration from time to time. The computer gave him access to any kind of research he might need, as well as a place to write his article.

The thunderstorm had moved off to the east, the rain had let up, but the power was still out. Mark decided that since he was already up, it would be a good time to get his morning walk in with Casey. It only made sense to check out the drive to his ranch house at the same time. If he got right on it, he might be able to prevent the drive from washing out.

After putting on his slicker and cowboy hat, he opened the door. As soon as the door opened, Casey came running back to the house. He was excited that his master was going for a walk.

Before leaving the house, Mark lit a Coleman lantern to take with him. He also took a shovel from along side the porch. He followed Casey out into the yard. He began by walking along the drive toward the paved road. The drive ran along the rim of the canyon for the first two hundred feet or so, then on to his ranch house. It was a fairly steep drop off in some places. On the other side, there were a few places where it was steep up the hill to the road above.

During his trek along the drive, he had found several places where the drive could wash out if it started to rain again. He fixed some of them by making a drainage ditch so the water would not build up and others by building small dikes to direct the run off in a different direction.

While he worked on the drive, Casey would run off into the darkness and then suddenly reappear. Casey seemed to enjoy the romp in the early morning darkness.

Just as Mark came around a sharp bend in the drive, he saw Casey near a small tree. The dog had apparently found something of interest. He was sniffing at something near the base of a tree. Mark held his lantern high in an effort to see what Casey found so interesting. Unable to see what it was, he started to walk toward the tree to get a better look.

At first, Mark thought it was a pile of rags or a bag of garbage. But when he got closer, he was surprised to find a woman curled up in a coat under the tree. Mark pushed his dog aside and he knelt down beside her.

"Get back, Casey."

Mark wasn't sure if the woman was even alive. He reached out and put his fingers along side the woman's neck. From the moment he touched her, she began to shiver.

She was still alive, but she was in serious condition.

"Ma'am," he said as he gently brushed a bunch of wet tangled hair out of the woman's face.

In the deep recesses of her mind, Lora thought she heard something, but it sounded like it was coming from a long way away. Her ability to think was impaired as a result of the accident, the pain that consumed her entire body, and the fact she was so cold she could do nothing but shiver. She had been drifting back and forth between semi-consciousness and unconsciousness.

As Mark touched her along side the face, she moved slightly and moaned as if his touch was painful to her. In a muffled, almost inaudible sound, he heard her pleading for help.

"Help me, please," she whispered.

"You're going to be all right," Mark said in the hope he was getting through to her, but he was not sure.

Mark held up the lantern to get a better look at her. He noticed the blood on the side of her head and in her hair. On closer examination, he discovered her left wrist was injured, and her right ankle was severely swollen. He had no idea if she had any internal injuries, but she was in immediate need of help.

It was obvious to Mark that what she was wearing was too lightweight for the weather. She had no shoes on and her nylons were ripped and torn. Everything she had on indicated she had been crawling in the mud. From the looks of her, she had been crawling for some distance.

If she were going to survive, it was up to him to get her someplace warm and dry. Mark was hesitant to move her for fear he might cause her more injury. But on the other hand, if he didn't move her, she would probably not survive much longer in the wet cold weather.

Mark took off his slicker and laid it on the ground beside her. He carefully picked her up and put her on his slicker and wrapped it around her. He then picked her up in his arms.

The woman had not responded to him until he adjusted her weight in his arms. At that moment she rested her head against his shoulder. Mark bent down and picked up the lantern.

"Come on, boy," Mark said as he started back to the ranch house.

It was a long walk back to his ranch house. Mark found the woman to be light in his arms. He was glad to see the rain had stopped and there was a hint of light in the eastern sky. It meant the sun would be up soon.

Several questions passed through Mark's mind as he carried her to his ranch house. He wondered what the woman was doing on his drive. Had she been dumped there after being attacked by some deranged person? Was she trying to get to his place? If she was, what did she want of him? He did not recognize her.

Once inside the ranch house, Mark laid the woman down on the floor in front of the fireplace. He lit a couple of storm lanterns and set them on the mantel. Mark added several pieces of wood to the smoldering embers in the fireplace to get the fire going again. It almost immediately burst into flames giving off light as well as its warmth.

Unable to make contact with the outside world, Mark knew he would have to draw on his experience from the military as a Naval Hospital corpsman. The first thing he needed to do was to get her out of her wet clothes and get her warm.

Mark got a large comforter from his bedroom and spread it out on the floor next to the woman. After removing the slicker from around her, he removed her wet and muddy coat. He found she had on a very expensive and very nice looking dress. At least it had been at one time. It was now torn and muddy.

He removed her wet dress, but left her in her bra and panties even though they were wet. He also removed her ripped and torn nylons, then picked her up and moved her onto the comforter, quickly wrapping her up in it.

Mark gathered a washcloth, soap and a couple of towels from the bathroom. He heated some water. As soon as it was ready, he took it into the living room and set it on the floor next to the woman.

Being as careful as he could to avoid making her injuries worse, Mark began washing the dirt and blood from her face. He quickly discovered she was a very pretty woman. She had a deep gash at her hairline above her right eye. He was sure it should have a couple of stitches in it, but he was not equipped to do it. Instead he made a butterfly bandage to close the wound then put a gauze dressing over it.

He then uncovered her legs enough to wash the dirt and mud off her legs and ankles. He carefully examined her right ankle in an effort to determine if her ankle was broken or badly sprained. It was impossible to tell with all the swelling. The only sure way to know would be to have her ankle x-rayed. Her ankle was already beginning to turn black and blue.

He wrapped her ankle in an ice pack and elevated it to help reduce the swelling. He tucked a pillow under her leg and covered her with the comforter.

Mark washed her left wrist and examined it as well. He couldn't find anything broken, but again, there was no way for him to be sure. At least if it was broken, it was not a compound fracture. Like her ankle, it was already swollen and turning black and blue.

He wrapped her wrist in an ice pack, elevated it and put her arm on another pillow, again covering her up with the comforter.

Mark checked her for any other injuries while he washed her as best he could. When he was finished, he looked up at her face. She was still in a semi-conscious state. From the look on her face, it was clear she was in pain, but there was nothing he could do about it. He wished he could do more for her, but he had no idea what the total extent of her injuries might be. From the cut on her head, she could have a severe head injury or maybe a concussion. To move her any more than necessary would be to risk more injury to her. There was always the possibility of some internal injuries.

He gathered some more pillows and the cushions from the sofa then packed them around her to keep her from moving. There was nothing more he could do but to keep her quiet, not allow her to move too much and keep her as comfortable as possible, at least until he could get some medical help for her.

Mark sat down on the floor beside her and kept a close watch over her. He took hold of her good wrist to check her pulse. It was good, much improved since he found her. Mark spent the next half hour watching her and checking her pulse every ten minutes to make sure she was stable. The fact that her vital signs remained stable was encouraging.

Although the color in her face seemed to have improved slightly since he first brought her into his house, she continued to drift in and out of consciousness. Mark decided it would be best to just let her rest as best she could for now. There was nothing more he could do until the telephone lines were repaired and he could call out. It was the first time that he actually thought about getting a cell phone, although he didn't know if it would work in the kind of weather they had been having lately.

Mark gathered up the towels, washcloth and wash bowl and took them to the bathroom where he rinsed them out and hung them up to dry. He could wash them later.

When Mark returned to the living room, he found the woman resting much more peacefully. He was sure the ice packs around her wrist and ankle were helping to reduce the pain as well as the swelling. Mark found Casey was lying beside her with his head on one of the cushions. He seemed to be watching over her, too.

"That's a good boy. You keep an eye on her," Mark said as he smiled at Casey.

Casey raised his head up off the cushion, looked up at his master then laid his head back down again.

Having done all he could for the woman, it was now time for Mark to look out for himself. He was still in his wet clothes. He decided it would be okay to leave her for a few minutes. Her vital signs were stable and she was showing signs of getting a little rest. That was the best thing for her right now.

Mark went into the bathroom, stripped out of his wet clothes and stepped into a luke warm shower. While in the shower, he tried to think of ways he might be able to help the woman. With the power out, it would be awhile before he could notify any emergency personnel.

He thought about putting her in his pickup truck and taking her to the hospital, but decided against it. There were two things he knew he didn't want to do if at all possible. The first was he shouldn't move her any more than necessary. To do so could make her injuries worse. He had already moved her more than he wanted to, but in this case not moving her would have been worse.

The second was not to leave her alone for more than a few minutes at a time. The best things he could do for her right now would be to keep her warm, keep her from moving too much and keep her as comfortable as possible until he could get in touch with the outside world.

After a quick shower and a set of clean clothes, Mark went back into the living room. He took a few minutes to check her vital signs to make sure she had not worsened. Relieved to find them still stable, he sat down in a rocking chair near the fire where he could watch her.

Hundreds of questions continued to cross his mind over and over again as he slowly rocked back and forth while watching her. He knew none of his questions would be answered until she was awake and talking, and only then if she wished to tell him.

He glanced out the window and noticed the sun was starting to come up over the horizon. He liked this time of the morning.

It often made for the most spectacular view of beautiful sunrises. The colors were gorgeous from his bedroom window, too.

He looked again at the woman lying on the floor. As the sun began to creep in the window, he realized it would soon be shining on her face. She needed her rest more than she needed to see the sunrise. She didn't need the sun waking her up.

Mark walked across the room and pulled the curtains closed to shut out the morning light. He heard her moan and turned to look at her. She moved only slightly then seemed to doze off again.

Mark tiptoed back across the room. He knelt down, lifted the comforter and took hold of her wrist. Her pulse was steady and seemed to be a little stronger.

After tucking her hand back under the comforter, he took a moment to check the phone to see if it was working. It was not; so he returned to his rocking chair. He looked over at her for a moment or two before closing his eyes to think. His experience as a hospital corpsman while in the Navy told him that she would probably go in and out of sleep for most of the day.

It had been a long night for Mark and he needed some rest, too. He pulled an afghan over himself and swung his feet up onto the footstool, then tipped back and closed his eyes.

Lora opened her eyes and found it to be dark except for the flickering of light from the fireplace. She did not know where she was, but she was warm and dry. Lora was still very much aware of the pain in her ankle and wrist, but somehow it didn't seem to be as severe as she remembered. She again closed her eyes and let herself drift off to sleep.

When she woke again, her mind was a little clearer and she was able to think. She could remember bits and pieces of what had happened. Her wrist and ankle throbbed, but the pain was at least tolerable as long as she didn't try to move too much.

She turned her head as she looked around the room. There was nothing familiar about it. Suddenly, her eyes caught sight of a large dog. It startled her and she tensed a little which caused a sudden shooting pain to run threw her wrist. The dog's big head was only inches from her face. Since the dog did not move, she realized the dog must be sleeping. She could not remember ever having seen the dog before.

She slowly turned her head the other way. Lora could see a man sleeping in a rocker. It was too dark for her to see him clearly, but she was sure she had never met him before. Again, she closed her eyes and drifted off to sleep.

When she opened her eyes again, she looked toward the rocker. The man was gone. She turned her head the other way and discovered the dog was gone, too. She wondered if she had been dreaming.

She closed her eyes as she tried to remember what had happened last night. As she began to piece together the events of last evening, she remembered seeing someone in the rain and darkness. She also remembered the feeling of being lifted up. She wondered if whoever it was had brought her to this place. The more she thought about it, the more she realized there was no other way she could have gotten there alone.

As the events of last night became more understandable in her mind, she began to remember seeing Jeff in the arms of his secretary. That thought seemed to cause her more pain than her injuries. Tears once again welled up in her eyes as the feeling of betrayal filled her thoughts. She began to cry openly, unable to contain the pain she felt in her heart.

Mark had gone to the kitchen to make coffee and to let Casey outside for a little while. He was thinking about the woman in his living room, but his thoughts were interrupted by the sound of crying. He quickly moved to where he could see her. The woman had not moved very much, but she was crying. His first thought was she was in pain from her injuries, but somehow that didn't strike him as being the case.

Mark stepped out of the kitchen and into the living room. He wasn't sure she even knew he was there.

"How are you feeling?" Mark spoke softly hoping he wouldn't frighten her.

She quickly turned her head and looked up at him. She could not see his face very well with the light behind him and the tears in her eyes, but she could see he was tall with broad shoulders.

"How are you feeling?" he asked again.

"Who are you?" she asked.

He thought he detected a hint of fear in her voice.

"I'm sorry to disturb you, but," he stopped before he said anything more. "I'm sorry, my name is Mark Howard. I live here. What is your name?"

She hesitated for a moment. Lora knew her name, she just wasn't sure she should tell him. She was afraid of this tall dark stranger, but she didn't know why. If he had been the one to help her, she owed him her life.

"Lora," she replied in a whisper.

"Do you have a last name, Lora?"

"Winters, Lora Winters."

"Well, Lora Winters, you've had quite a night. Do you think you can tell me how you managed to be on my drive?"

"On your drive?" she asked, a little confused by his comment.

"Yes," he replied, then waited for her to answer him.

Lora turned her head away. She wasn't sure how much she wanted to tell him. He was concerned about her, but she didn't know him. And her personal life was really none of his business. What was this about his drive?

"Well, that's all right. It's probably best if you just rest for awhile. As soon as I can make a call out, I'll get someone up here to take you to the hospital where you can get proper care," he said in an effort to reassure her that she would be all right.

She didn't respond, but closed her eyes. Lora turned in time to see him disappear into the kitchen. She knew she should have at least thanked him for helping her, but her world had been turned upside down and not just because of the accident.

Lora tried to relax as best she could. Her wrist and ankle were still throbbing. Resting quietly with her eyes closed seemed to be the only thing that helped dull the pain.

When she opened her eyes again, she realized she must have dozed off because the curtains were now open. From where she was lying, she could see out the window. She could see the tops of the mountain ridges in the distance. The sky was clear and a bright blue. It was a nice view, but Mark disturbed her thoughts as he walked in from the kitchen. She turned and looked up at him.

"The phone lines are open again. I was able to get hold of the Sheriff's Office. There will be a helicopter on its way in a little while," Mark explained.

"A helicopter?" she said with surprise.

"Yes. I figured it was the fastest way to get you to a hospital where you can get proper medical care. I did the best I could with what I had, but you really need medical attention."

"Oh," she said as if she was disappointed, then turned her head and looked toward the fireplace.

Mark couldn't understand her reaction. It was almost as if she didn't want to leave. One minute she was afraid to talk to him. The next, she didn't seem to want to leave.

Mark walked over to the sliding glass door leading out to the porch. He opened the door and stepped outside. He was watching for the helicopter.

Lora turned and watched him. She wondered if he was looking for the helicopter or if he was simply enjoying the view.

She noticed he suddenly straightened up and looked off to the left. It was at about the same time that she heard the sound of a helicopter approaching. She could not see it, but she could see Mark was watching it as it landed in front of the house.

"I'll be right back," he said as he walked past her.

Mark walked through the house to the front door. He opened the door to allow several people into the house. One of them was a woman with a black bag. Two men with a gurney and other medical equipment followed her. Mark didn't say anything to them, he simply pointed at Lora.

"Hi. I'm Doctor Julie Holm. How are you feeling?" she asked as she knelt down on the floor beside Lora.

"Not very well, I guess. My ankle and wrist hurt pretty bad."

"We'll take care of that. Do you hurt anywhere else?" the doctor asked as she took Lora's blood pressure.

"No. I don't think so."

"We'll get you to a hospital very shortly."

Mark stood out of the way while the doctor checked Lora's vital signs. When the doctor was finished examining her, the men lifted her off the floor and laid her on the gurney. They covered her with a blanket and strapped her in before wheeling her out the front door. Mark followed along behind and watched as Lora was placed in the helicopter.

"Say, is she going to be all right?" Mark asked the doctor.

"I think so. Do you know how she got here?"

"No. I found her on the drive late last night. I have no idea how she got there, and she hasn't bothered to tell me. She seems very frightened, but then I guess I can't blame her. It was a pretty nasty night up here last night."

"Why didn't you call us earlier?"

"The phones were out and I don't have a cell phone," he replied. "Maybe I should think about getting one."

"Maybe," the doctor said with a smile. "You did a good job of taking care of her injuries. How is it you knew what to do for her?"

"I was a hospital corpsman in the Navy."

"She should be glad you were," the doctor said with a smile.

"I hope she'll be okay."

"I think she will be fine now. I've got to go," Doctor Holm said.

Mark simply nodded and stepped back away from the helicopter as the doctor got in. The engine began to rev up and the helicopter lifted off the ground. He stood back and watched as the helicopter turned and moved off across the valley toward Denver. He watched until it was out of sight. As soon as it was gone, he went back into the ranch house.

CHAPTER THREE

Shortly after the helicopter set down on the heliport at the hospital in Denver, Lora was rushed into the receiving ward. A medical team, including doctors and nurses, examined her. Since her vital signs were stable, she was taken to x-ray where her wrist and ankle were x-rayed.

They put her ankle and wrist in soft casts to prevent any movement while keeping pressure from the swelling to a minimum. She was then admitted and taken to a hospital room where she could rest. It had been a long morning for Lora. It was almost noon by the time they had finished poking and prodding at her and getting her settled in a room.

Once in the room, she was given medication to help her sleep. As soon as the door to her room closed behind the last nurse to attend to her, she let her eyes close and she let out a long sigh. After all the hustle and bustle and the poking and prodding, she was feeling very tired. And now that everyone had left, she was feeling very much alone.

Lora had been given a sedative and was beginning to feel a bit groggy. Her mind tried to go over what had happened to her, but the medication kept her from thinking clearly. Only small bits and pieces of last night would come to mind then quickly fade away leaving her confused and a little disorientated, but she was no longer in pain. She continued to drift in and out of sleep for some time.

As the day went by, she thought of Mark several times. She was feeling a little guilty for not at least thanking him for saving her. Even in her clouded mind, she was able to understand he had saved her life.

She also thought of Jeff from time to time, but they were not pleasant thoughts. Every time she thought of him, she could picture him in the arms of his secretary. And every time she pictured him in her mind, she would cry.

It was not until after dinner that evening she was able to sleep. She found she was not able to sleep for very long at a time, however. She would often wake up and start to cry again before drifting back to sleep.

The sounds of the helicopter had long since faded away and Mark had gone back inside his ranch house. He was feeling rather tired after such a long morning, but his mind was too occupied with thoughts of Lora Winters for him to lie down and get any real rest. She had come into his life in the middle of a thunderstorm, but thoughts of her were not leaving his mind so quickly.

Mark walked over to his sofa and stretched out on it with the hope of getting some rest. As hard as he tried, he could not find sleep. There were too many unanswered questions going through his mind. It wasn't long before he simply gave up trying. He went to his desk for a little while in the hope of getting some work done, but quickly found he couldn't concentrate on it, either.

Since he didn't seem to have any control over his mind at the moment, Mark simply gave up. He leaned back in his chair and let his mind wander as it wanted. He could easily visualize Lora in his mind's eye. She was a pretty woman in spite of the fact she was dirty, wet and injured when he found her.

He once again looked at the computer screen in front of him and decided it would be better if he didn't even try to work. Instead, he decided to take a walk along the drive in an effort to see if he could find some of the answers to his questions. With that thought in mind, he reached up and turned off his computer and got up.

As he started for the door, he reached out, took his cowboy hat off the peg, put it on and opened the door. Since Casey never missed on opportunity to go for a walk with his master, he was at the door almost before Mark could get it opened.

Mark followed Casey outside. Casey danced around in front of Mark as he looked down the drive toward where he had found Lora. Casey seemed to have a pretty good idea where they were going and took off down the drive at a run.

The sun was shining and the clouds had long since disappeared. It was a beautiful day for a walk. Mark started off down the drive in the direction Casey had gone. He was not paying any attention to Casey. He was thinking about Lora Winters.

It didn't take him long before he came to the tree where Casey had found Lora. His shovel was still there. As he walked over to his shovel, he could envision the way she looked last night, curled up in a fetal position, shivering and wet, lying under the tree.

Mark began to study the surrounding area, especially the area around the base of the tree. With the heavy rains last night, all the tracks had been pretty much washed away. There was nothing left to indicate how she had gotten there.

As he looked around, Mark noticed Casey was down the drive a little way and was standing close to the edge of the drive. Casey had his head down and his tail out straight as if he were pointing at something. He was looking down into the canyon. Mark wondered what Casey had found so interesting. He walked down the drive to where Casey was and looked over the edge of the drive. He was trying to see what Casey was looking at so intently.

"What do you see, old boy?" Mark asked as he patted the dog on the head.

Mark stood beside Casey and studied the canyon for several minutes, but saw nothing from where he stood. He started walking along the edge of the drive, still looking into the canyon. It could have been a ground squirrel or some other small animal running around among the rocks that caught Casey's attention for all Mark knew.

Not far from where the drive turned and wandered up to the paved road above, Mark noticed a small tree at the edge of the drive. It was laid over and sort of pointed down the steep canyon wall. The damaged tree looked as if had been freshly broken off. He had not noticed the damaged tree yesterday about noontime when he had been out with Casey.

The tree looked more like it had been run over by something very heavy than knocked over in a storm. He slowly turned around and looked across the drive at the side of the hill. His gaze slowly turned up toward the paved road above the steep embankment. He noticed other small trees and some of the bushes on the embankment looked as if they had been pushed over as well.

Mark moved closer and looked up the side of the hill. He noticed the afternoon sun was reflecting off something shiny lying in among the damaged bushes. He couldn't make out what it was from where he was standing.

He began climbing up the steep embankment toward the object. When Mark got close to it, he pushed the bushes covering it aside. He discovered it was a small mirror. When he picked it up, he saw it was an outside rearview mirror from a car, or at least what was left of it.

Mark turned and looked back down the hill. He instantly realized what had happened. A car had rolled down the hill, across the narrow drive and on down into the canyon. He returned to his drive then hurried over to the edge. Casey stood beside him as Mark looked down into the canyon. He carefully scanned the bottom of the canyon. Below, he could barely make out what looked like the remains of a car. The only thing that led him to believe it was a car was it was upside down. He could make out the general lines of the frame. There were no wheels on the car, but then there was not much of it left.

"She must have gone off the road and rolled into the canyon," he said to Casey as if the dog would understand him.

As he continued to look down at the remains of the car, he became amazed at what he was seeing. There appeared to be nothing left of it but a mangled mess of scrap metal. Looking at the remains of the car, he found it hard to believe anyone could have survived such a wreck, let alone crawl back up to his drive.

Mark began to realize no one could have survived a wreck like that. If this was the car Lora had been in, she must have been thrown out of it at some point as it rolled down the steep embankment. She probably got out or was thrown out on the narrow ledge he could see just a little way down the canyon wall, he thought.

It suddenly occurred to Mark that there was a possibility that someone could still be in the car. With the way Lora Winters was dressed, she might have been out on a date. Her date could still be in the car.

That thought made his heart race. There was no question in his mind he had to find out. There was very little chance anyone could have survived if they were still in the car, but he would not be satisfied until he knew for sure.

"I hope there's no one else down there," Mark said more to himself than to Casey.

"Stay, boy," Mark commanded as he started down the steep incline.

Mark slowly and carefully picked his way down the side of the canyon wall. When he got to the ledge, he noticed deep scratches in the rocks as well as fresh oil stains. He paused only briefly before he began working his way around and over the rocks, on past the narrow ledge and down to the car.

When he finally got to the car, he hesitated. He was not sure what he would find once he looked inside. Holding his breath and silently praying there was no one in the car, he bent down and leaned close to the car as he looked inside. He let out a sigh of relief when he found the car was empty.

Mark sat down on a rock and looked back up toward the drive. He could see Casey looking over the edge and watching him, impatient to follow, yet obedient to his master.

Looking back at the car, he could not remember ever seeing a car that was so totally and completely destroyed except for one that had been crushed in a machine designed to crush automobiles. It was almost impossible for him to tell what kind of a car it had been.

After looking the car over, he reached inside the car and pried the glove compartment open. He found the papers on the car and removed them. He opened the packet of papers and found the registration slip and insurance card. Both showed the car was registered to Lora L. Winters of Denver.

He took a moment to look at the car again then looked back up the canyon wall. He shook his head in disbelief. It was impossible for him to believe she could have survived such an accident. She had to have escaped from the car at some point up the canyon wall for her to still be alive. From where he was standing there would have been no way she could have crawled all the way back up to his road where he found her with the injuries she had suffered.

Mark took one last look at the car then tucked the papers from the car into his pocket. He started climbing back up the canyon.

Just as Mark got back to the drive to the ranch house, he saw a Sheriff's patrol car turn onto his drive. He stopped and waited for the car to pull up to him. The car stopped and a tall lean man in a Sheriff's Deputy Uniform swung open the car door and got out.

"Hi," the deputy said casually.

"Hi," Mark replied.

"Are you Mark Howard?"

"Yes. I would guess you're here to talk to me about Lora Winters."

"That's right. What can you tell me about her?"

"Not much, I'm afraid. I can tell you that she is one very lucky lady. The car in the bottom of the canyon belongs to her," Mark said as he pointed to the place where the car had gone over the edge.

The deputy looked at Mark, then walked over to the edge of the drive and looked down. He just shook his head and turned back toward Mark.

"Are you sure that's her car?"

"Yes. Here's the registration and insurance card," Mark said as he held them out to the deputy.

"You climbed down there?" the deputy asked with a note of surprise and disbelief in his voice.

"Yes. How else was I going to find out if anyone was still in the car?"

"Right. Is there anyone else in the car?"

"No."

"Any ideas as to how it happened?"

"Not really, but my best guess would be she lost control of the car on the curve up there," Mark said as he pointed toward the paved road above them.

The deputy looked up the hill, then turned back and looked at Mark.

"I understand you found her last night. What were you doing out in the storm?"

"I actually found her early this morning. The storm was almost over. But to answer your question, I was checking my drive to make sure it was not washing out. It's pretty narrow in some places and we've had a lot of rain lately."

"That we have," the deputy agreed. "Where did you find Miss Winters?"

"Less than a hundred feet down there," Mark replied as he pointed toward the tree where he had found her curled up.

"Why don't you show me," the deputy suggested.

"Sure."

They started walking toward the tree where Mark had found Lora. The deputy looked around as they walked. Casey ran on ahead and waited for them near the tree.

"I found her right here," Mark said as he pointed at the base of the tree.

The deputy walked over and looked around under the tree. It looked to Mark as if he was looking for something, a clue or a hint as to what happened and how she got there. He then looked back to where the car had gone over the edge and down into the canyon.

"This is a long way from where the car went over. How do you suppose she got here?"

"I don't know, but my guess would be she crawled over here. She must have been one determined woman," Mark added.

"Yeah, she would have to have been to get this far."

"By the way, do you know how she is doing?" Mark asked.

"Last I heard she was resting well in the hospital. We have not been able to talk to her, yet."

"Why is that? She seemed able to talk when she was here."

"She has been put under some fairly heavy sedation. I'm sure this experience has been rather traumatic for her."

"I'm sure it has been," Mark replied as he thought about Lora and her injuries.

He had to wonder if her injuries were more severe than he had thought. Otherwise, why would she be under heavy sedation? The only reason he could think of was so she could get some rest. He was also sure her injured ankle and wrist were probably very painful. Those thoughts seemed to ease his mind a little.

"You think maybe someone left her here, then ran her car off into the canyon?" the deputy asked as he looked at Mark.

"Why would anyone do that?"

"I was hoping you could tell me."

Mark looked at the deputy. The deputy seemed to be looking to Mark for answers, but Mark didn't have any answers. All he had were the same questions the deputy was asking him.

"How would I know?"

"Just wondering if you might have some ideas as to what happened to her."

"Like I said, I don't know what happened," Mark said, as he looked the deputy in the eyes.

"Do you think she might have been beaten?"

"Not from the looks of her injuries."

"Oh," the deputy said as he looked at Mark with some interest. "Are you some kind of an expert on injuries?"

"No, but I have had some experience."

"How's that?"

"I was a medic in the service."

"Oh," the deputy said thoughtfully. "How did she get to your house?"

Mark was getting a little concerned with where the deputy's questions seemed to be leading. He seemed to be going over the same ground again and again, and adding a little each time. Mark was so engrossed in his thoughts he didn't really hear what the deputy had asked him.

"What? I'm sorry, I didn't hear what you asked."

"I asked how did she get from here to your house?"

"I carried her to the house."

"You carried her?" he asked, squinting his eyes as he looked at Mark.

"Yes, I carried her," Mark repeated, a little disgusted that he had to repeat himself.

The deputy looked at Mark, then looked off toward the house. He felt it was a long way to carry someone.

Mark thought about saying something, but decided against it. At the time, he was more concerned about Lora's well being than anything else.

"Why did you move her from here? Wasn't that a little risky considering her injuries?"

"I suppose you could say that, but I believed if I had left her here in the rain, she might very well have died from exposure helped along by her injuries. It was a choice I had to make at the time. I chose to take her to my house, which, by the way, is the closest place that was warm and dry."

"You're pretty sure that moving her was the best thing to do?"

"Nothing is for sure. In my opinion, it was the best thing to do under the circumstances and at the time."

"In your opinion?"

"Yes, in my opinion. I'm sorry if you disagree, but I didn't have anyone else to consult with at the time, so I moved her," Mark replied a little harsher than he had intended.

This deputy was starting to get on his nerves.

"Why did you wait so long to call for help?"

Mark took a deep breath. He had to take a second to get hold of his temper before he answered. He was getting a little tired of the deputy's apparent innuendoes. He was getting the feeling the deputy was about to accuse him of something, but he had no idea of what.

"The power was out and my phone wasn't working. I can only assume the phone lines were down. I called out as soon as I was able. And before you ask, I don't have a cell phone," Mark replied with a little more control of his voice.

"Do you know Miss Winters?"

"No. I never saw her before this morning."

"Are you sure you never met her before. Maybe in an office building, in a park, at her apartment, or maybe at a party," the deputy suggested as he looked at Mark.

"No. I never met the woman before. I have no idea where she lives or where she is from."

"You're sure?"

"Yes, I'm sure. I didn't know where she lived until I saw the registration to her car just a little while ago."

"What do you think she was doing up here?"

"You've already asked me that and I told you. I have no idea why she was up here. She didn't bother to tell me," Mark replied, his voice once again beginning to show he was getting tired of this deputy's approach.

The way the deputy looked at him, and the way he asked his questions, seemed to indicate to Mark that he was looking for something more from him. Maybe even someone to blame.

"You sure she wasn't coming up here to see you?"

"What makes you think that?"

"She was dressed in a rather, shall we say, revealing dress."

"So? That doesn't mean she was coming to see me."

"Then how would you explain it?"

"I wouldn't. I have no idea what she was doing, what her plans were, or where she was going, or for that matter where she had been."

"I see," the deputy said.

"I doubt that. Look. If you have something to say, say it. Otherwise, I have better things to do."

"I'm just trying to find out what happened up here," the deputy said with a slight grin.

"Like I said before, I don't know what happened. If you want to know that, I'd suggest you ask Miss Winters," Mark said sharply.

With that, Mark turned on his heels and began walking to his ranch house. Casey quickly joined him. Mark was about to lose his temper over the insinuations the deputy had made by the way he stated his questions. Mark had had enough and wasn't going to put up with any more.

"Mr. Howard," the deputy called out.

Mark stopped in his tracks then slowly turned around. He did not respond. Instead, he just looked at the deputy.

"I'll be back to talk to you again," the deputy said with a grin.

"I'll bet you will," Mark said under his breath so the deputy couldn't hear him.

Mark thought about telling the deputy that if he came back he had better have a warrant, but decided against it. Mark had nothing to hide from the authorities. The last thing he wanted to do was to have any problems with them. If this deputy came to talk to him again and continued the same line of questioning, he would take some action at that time. For now, he would try to mind his own business.

Mark stood in the middle of the drive and watched as the deputy walked back to his car. Casey had come up beside him and sat down next to his master. After the deputy had gone, Mark reached down and scratched the dog's head as he thought about the deputy's attitude toward him. It bothered Mark, but there was nothing he could do about it now.

Mark watched the deputy drive away, then turned and went into the ranch house. He walked through the house and out onto the porch overlooking the valley. Mark's thoughts turned back to Lora.

The deputy had not asked him any questions he had not wanted the answers to himself, but that was not the problem. The problem was the way the deputy asked them. Mark had gotten the impression the deputy thought Mark had caused Lora's injuries or at least was responsible for them somehow. There was certainly a possibility someone was involved. However, the injuries Lora had received were not the kind of injuries one would expect to see on someone who had been beaten.

Mark knew that there was always the possibility Lora had been forced off the road. It seemed rather unlikely given the loneliness of the area, but it was possible. It seemed more likely she had been driving too fast for the weather conditions. She would not be the first one to slide off the road in bad weather. She was the first one to roll a car into the canyon, however. There could have been something on the road she tried to avoid causing her to lose control and go over the edge.

The one thing that Mark wondered about was why she was on the road in the first place. There were very few homes out this way. There were only four other small ranches on past the curve. Two of those ranches were nothing more than hobby ranches. They belonged to people who lived in the city and only came up on the weekends.

Then there was the McDonnell's ranch, but they spent most of their time in the city. They hardly came up to the ranch at all anymore. And then there was the old man's ranch about a half mile up the road from where Lora went off the road.

Mark had heard the old man died last winter. Mark had never been to the old man's ranch house by the road. He had always cut across the pasture to visit him. Mark tried to remember what the old man's last name was, but he couldn't remember if he had ever heard it. He knew him simply as Wilbur.

Mark had never seen anyone around the place, but he couldn't watch it every minute. He had been sort of keeping an eye on the place to prevent vandals from causing damage to it, but that was only because it was close to his own ranch.

He began to wonder if Lora had been trying to go somewhere along the road, or if she had gotten lost in the storm. Getting lost might explain why she was on the road. It also might explain why she lost it on the curve. If she didn't know the road, she might have misjudged the curve and slid off the wet slippery pavement.

He knew there would be no answers to his questions unless he could see Lora and ask her. It was that thought that made him turn around and go back inside.

He walked through the house then went out to the barn to make sure his horses had food and water. He turned them out into the paddock and went to work cleaning their stalls. When he was finished, he returned to the house.

After a quick shower and shave, he changed into casual clothes. Before leaving, he put out a bowl of food and fresh water for Casey. He got into his truck and headed for Denver to see Lora.

CHAPTER FOUR

When Mark arrived in Denver, he stopped off at a local restaurant for a meal before going on to the hospital. After parking his truck in the parking lot at the hospital, he went inside and inquired about Lora.

"Excuse me, but could you tell me where I might find Miss Lora Winters?" he asked of the desk attendant.

The receptionist looked through the files and then looked up at him. From the look on her face, he wasn't sure if she was going to tell him her room number.

"She's on the third floor. You will need to check with the floor nurse to see if she can have visitors."

"Thank you," he replied, then walked to the elevators.

Mark pressed the button then waited for the elevator. When it arrived, he stepped inside. As the doors closed, he could see the receptionist watching him from behind her desk. The way the receptionist looked at him and the way he had been questioned by the deputy made him wonder if maybe he was getting involved in something he would prefer to stay out of.

As the elevator ascended, Mark began to wonder if paying a visit to Lora was such a good idea. He really didn't know Miss Winters. He wasn't even sure if she would want to see him. The whole thing could be embarrassing for her and might prove to be trouble for him, although he didn't know what kind of trouble it could mean to him. After all, he had done nothing but try to help her.

Suddenly, his thoughts were disturbed by the elevator door opening. He stood motionless as he looked out at the nurse's station. It wasn't until the doors began to close that he made up his mind to get off the elevator. Mark quickly reached out and stopped the doors from closing, then stepped off the elevator and walked up to the nurse's station. He waited for the woman behind the counter to say something.

"May I help you?" the woman asked as she looked up at Mark.

"I was wondering if Miss Lora Winters was up to having a visitor."

The expression on the nurse's face suddenly changed. Her eyes narrowed slightly as she looked at him. He immediately began to wonder what was going on. For a moment or so he was not sure if she was going to let him visit her. He wondered what difference it made to her.

"Are you her boyfriend?" she asked, her eyes looking him over with a hint of suspicion.

The thought that she had a boyfriend sent a strange feeling through Mark. He had not thought of that possibility. Mark wasn't sure how he felt about visiting her now. His first clear thought was to leave. He didn't want to cause any friction between Lora and her boyfriend.

Mark's second thought was what difference it could make to the nurse if he was Lora's boyfriend or not. Maybe they were only letting her family and her boyfriend in to see her, he thought.

"No. I was the one who found her after the accident. I was simply interested in how she is doing."

"What is your name?"

"Mark Howard."

"Wait here, please. I'll see if she's awake," the nurse said as she stood up.

Mark watched as the nurse started down the hall. He was puzzled by her response to his answer. Maybe it was the boyfriend they were trying to keep away from her, but that didn't seem to make any sense to Mark.

He watched as the nurse disappeared into a room. In no more than a minute or so the nurse returned and started walking toward him.

"She will see you. Room three-twenty-one," she said with a smile.

Mark nodded a brief thank you and started down the hall. As he came closer to her door, he couldn't think of what to say to her. He had wanted to visit her and find out what happened, but now that he was here what was he going to say to her.

He hesitated a moment at the door and glanced back toward the nurse's station. He saw that the nurse was watching him. He forced a bit of a smile, then turned toward the door.

Mark lightly knocked on the door to Lora's room.

"Come in," a soft voice from inside said.

Mark pushed the door open and peered around it. Lora was lying on the hospital bed. The head of the bed was up a little and she had pillows behind her head. He noticed her ankle was in a cast and propped up on a pillow. Her wrist was also in a cast and propped up on another pillow laid across her lap.

"I hope I am not disturbing you," Mark said as he stepped into the room.

"No. Not at all. Come in, please," she said with a smile.

"How are you doing?"

"Pretty good, I guess."

"Looks like you will be laid up for awhile," Mark said as he stepped up closer to the bed and looked at the casts.

"Yes. I will have the casts on for about six weeks."

"Oh."

"Have the police talked to you yet?"

"Yes," Mark replied with a grin. "A deputy sheriff stopped by my place and asked me a lot of questions that I couldn't answer. Mostly about what happened and a few about you."

"I'm terribly sorry. I hope they didn't accuse you of, well, anything wrong."

"The deputy didn't actually accuse me of anything, but he hinted that I might have been involved in your accident in some way," Mark said with a smile in an effort to show he wasn't upset or concerned about it.

Mark watched her as she turned away from him and looked toward the window. He wondered what she was thinking, and what he had said that made her turn away.

Slowly, she turned back and looked at him. Mark thought he could see tears in her beautiful brown eyes. He hoped he had not caused her to cry.

"Are you all right?" he asked. "Do you need a nurse?"

"I'm sorry. I guess I'm still a little shook up over the accident. The medication they have been giving me for pain makes me kind of sleepy."

"That's certainly understandable," he said as he thought about the way her car looked in the bottom of the canyon.

"Maybe, I should go and let you get your rest," he added as he stood up.

"I'm sorry. I'm having a hard time dealing with all this right now."

"It's all right," he replied with a slight smile. "Would it be all right with you if I come see you again, maybe in a day or two when you are feeling better?"

It had not been Mark's intention to see her again. He had come to find out if she was going to be okay, then simply drop out of her life. Something deep inside had let the words sort of slip out.

"Yes, I guess it would be all right. I'll be here for at least a week, they tell me."

"Is there anything you need, or anything I can get for you?"

"No. I have everything I need, but thanks for asking."

"Okay. I'll stop in again before you go home. If there's anything you need or anything that I can do for you, just call me. That is if you want to. I'll leave you my phone number in case you need something."

She watched Mark as he took a piece of paper out of his pocket and wrote down his phone number on it. He put the paper on her bedside table, and then smiled at her.

Lora smiled at him, then watched him as he turned and walked toward the door. As soon as he stepped out into the hall and disappeared, she leaned back and stared at the door as if she was waiting for him to turn around and come back in, but he didn't.

She looked over at the piece of paper with his number on it and wondered if she would ever hear from him again. It was a nice gesture on his part, but she was sure he didn't really expect her to call him.

Lora tipped her head back and closed her eyes. She wanted to sleep, but sleep would not come easy for her. No matter how hard she tried she could not get the picture of Jeff and his secretary out of her mind. Right now she was having a hard time dealing with it, to say nothing of her injuries.

She tried to think of Mark as a way to get Jeff off her mind, but it didn't work very well. What Jeff had done to her was too new, too traumatic and too close to her heart. She knew it would be awhile before she would be able to trust anyone again.

Mark walked on down the hall, stopping in front of the elevator. He pressed the button to summon the elevator. As he waited, he could picture Lora in the hospital bed, her wrist and ankle in casts, and a clean white dressing on her head where he had put a butterfly bandage. He couldn't help but notice how tired and weary she looked. He also remembered the tears in her eyes.

A picture of her car also came to mind, a twisted and crushed piece of metal, glass and plastic lying at the bottom of the canyon. He couldn't help but think about how very lucky she was to even be alive. In fact, she was so lucky to be alive he couldn't understand why she seemed to cry at the drop of pin. Maybe it was her reaction to having survived such a horrible accident.

The elevator doors opening suddenly disturbed Mark's thoughts. As Mark was about to step into the elevator, a man in a business suit came charging out and ran into him. Mark had to take a couple of quick steps backward to avoid falling over. The man rushed on by and didn't even have the decency to say, "Excuse me". The man seemed to be in an awfully big hurry, to say nothing of the fact that he was rude and careless.

Mark thought the least the inconsiderate individual could do was to apologize. He briefly thought about letting the guy know it, but decided not to press the issue. After all, he was probably here to see someone he was worried about. That was still no excuse for the man's rudeness, but it was a good reason for Mark to let it slide. The last thing Mark wanted was to cause the man more stress.

Mark stepped into the elevator and turned around. He could see the man leaning over the nurse's station counter. Mark could not hear what the man was saying, but it was clear he was demanding information about someone. The man had not only been rude, he was also pushy.

As the doors to the elevator closed, Mark thought he heard the man say, "What do you mean she won't see me?" Mark wasn't real sure what the man had said. Besides, it was none of his business.

Mark smiled to himself as he thought about the man. He was not going to get anywhere with the nurse on duty by yelling at her. In fact, he might find himself getting tossed out of the hospital by security.

He walked out of the hospital and across the parking lot to his truck. Mark was still thinking about how he had given Lora an opportunity to tell him what happened without coming right out and asking her. For some reason, she had chosen not to explain anything to him.

When Mark got to his truck, he got in and put the key in the ignition, but did not start the truck. Instead, he sat behind the steering wheel as he stared out the windshield at the hospital. There was something about this woman that intrigued him and captured his mind at the same time. She haunted his mind like no other woman he had known.

Mark shook his head, let out a sigh and started his truck. He knew whatever it was that caused him to be unable to get Lora off his mind would not be found in the parking lot. He drove out of the parking lot and onto the street. It wasn't long before he was out on the highway headed back toward the mountains.

Once on the road to his place, he couldn't stop wondering what had caused the accident. When Mark came to the turnoff to his place, he slowed down but he did not turn in. He continued on to the place where Lora's car had gone off the road, a little past the curve in the road to a wide place on the shoulder where he could get his truck off the road.

Mark got out and walked back down the road to where Lora's car had gone over the edge. He immediately noticed the shoulder of the road along the curve had washed out, right up to the edge of the pavement. As a result, the shoulder of the road was at least six inches below the pavement. It was clear to Mark that the minute the wheels of Lora's car slid off the pavement, she would have been unable to control the car. There would have been no stopping it from going over the edge.

The question became what caused her to get off the pavement in the first place? The pavement was wide enough that she should not have gone off onto the shoulder.

Whatever tell-tail signs there might have been had been washed away by the rain. There was no way of knowing what really happened unless Lora decided to talk about it.

Mark walked back to his truck. He stood at the door while he looked up the road.

What was up that way that would be of interest to her, he wondered.

He got back in his truck and drove on up the road for a little ways. Mark had no idea what he was looking for, but it wouldn't hurt to drive on a little further. It had been a long time since he had had any reason to be up that way.

As he came around another corner, the name on the side of a mailbox caught his attention and he hit the brakes. His truck came to a sudden stop in the middle of the road as he stared at the name on the mailbox. It read simply "W. W. Winters".

Mark wondered if she had been headed there when she went off the road. It certainly would seem to make sense. At least the last name was the same.

The man who had lived there had not been there for some time. He would come and stay in the house for most of the summer, but as soon as winter came he moved away to Arizona, if Mark remembered correctly.

Mark remembered the man was rather old and he walked with a cane, and his health had not been good for as long as Mark had known him. The last couple of times Mark had visited with the old man, he was sitting on the large back porch of the house.

Mark couldn't remember the old man's last name, but he did remember his first name. It was Wilbur. Was it possible Wilbur was a relative of Lora's? That seemed like a pretty strong possibility at the moment.

Mark pulled into the driveway and turned around. He then started back toward his own ranch house.

He knew the old man had died several months ago after a long illness. If he was a relative of Lora's, she might have been coming up to check on the place. But why would she do it in a fancy evening dress? And why would she be up here to check on the house in the middle of a nasty thunderstorm? Somehow it didn't make any sense to Mark.

Mark pulled up in front of his house and shut off the engine. As he got out of his truck, he looked over toward the old man's ranch house. He could see a little of it from his place, just a small corner of the house. He had not seen a light on in the house for several months, so he was pretty sure no one was living there.

Mark's mind took him back to the first time he had met the old man. It was a warm summer day when Mark was riding one of his horses in the U.S. Forest Service land behind the old man's ranch. He had come upon the old man while he was walking in the woods. That was over a year ago.

After their first meeting, Mark invited the old man to go riding with him a few times. On their rides they would talk about the old days when the old man was a young man. Sometimes they would talk about horses, and sometimes about the world in general and how it had changed over the past five to eight decades.

Mark had enjoyed listening to him, but the old man rarely talked about his family. He only talked about a granddaughter which he didn't see very often, but spoke fondly of her. Mark assumed that he didn't have any other family.

Mark finally went inside his ranch house, fixed himself a cup of coffee and sat down to think. After a while, Mark gave up trying to figure out what was going on and decided to take care of his horses then go to bed. Mark went out to the paddock and rounded up his horses. He put them in the barn, fed them and got them bedded down for the night.

After a quick shower, Mark climbed into bed. He lay with his hands behind his head looking up at the ceiling. He tried to clear his mind and get some sleep, but it was not easy. His mind was consumed with all the unanswered questions that ran around in his head. It was some time before he could clear his mind enough to get some sleep.

After Mark left Lora's room, Lora let out a long slow sigh. All she knew about him was the fact he had saved her life, and she found him to be kind and considerate. He was also very handsome, but then Jeff had been like that, too.

The thought of Jeff once again filled her eyes with tears. He had been kind and considerate to her all the time they had been going together. He had seemed like the perfect man for her. In her mind, he had been the one man she would want to share her life with and raise a family with. Yet, he had proven he could not be trusted with her most valuable possession, her heart.

For all Lora knew, Jeff might have other girlfriends around Denver. The one bright spot in the whole mess was she found out about him before she married him. In her mind, the minute he had asked her to marry him was when he should have stopped seeing any other woman. The fact she had found out about his infidelity did little to make her feel better.

At this moment, Lora was feeling very much alone. Her wrist and ankle were hurting a little even though she had been given something to dull the pain. The fact that the man she had loved had been unfaithful to her hurt her more than the injuries. The very happiness she had hoped for was now gone. It went like a puff a smoke. For the second time in her life she had been disappointed by a man.

She laid resting and looking toward the window. It was dark outside. The only things she could see were a few lights in the buildings nearby.

Lora began to think about what she was going to do now. She would not be able to return to work for several weeks because of her injuries. At least, money was not a problem for her as her grandfather had left her with a trust fund she could live on in relative comfort. She would not be able to return to her job of working with children at the public library, a job she enjoyed very much.

The fact that she lived alone was going to make it even more difficult for her. She could not think of one positive thing in her life at that moment.

Her thoughts about her immediate future were disturbed by the sound of voices coming from down the hall. She quickly recognized the loud male voice. It was Jeff. He was the last person she wanted to see. She had asked the nursing staff not to let him in to see her. It was beginning to look like she might not have a choice.

Lora turned and watched the door expecting Jeff to come barging into her room at any moment. With the medication and her emotions in turmoil, she was not ready to face him. She didn't think that she could stand to deal with him now.

The door to her room slowly started to open. Lora braced herself for a painful confrontation with Jeff. She let out a sigh of relief when she saw it was the nurse who had come in to check on her.

"Is he gone?" Lora asked, hoping he was.

"Yes, at least for now. He was very upset that you didn't want him to see you," the nurse said, her voice soft and understanding.

"I can't deal with him right now," Lora said as she turned and looked out the window.

"I had to threaten him with having security throw him out of the hospital before he would leave. He was very angry."

"I'm sorry. I'm sorry to put you through all this," she said as she turned and looked at the nurse.

"Did he hurt you?"

"Yes," Lora sighed.

"I can call the police so you can file charges against him," the nurse suggested.

"No. He hurt me, but he didn't do this to me," she said as she glanced at her casts.

"What did happen? You know the police are going to want to know."

"If you don't mind, I'd rather not talk about it. I'll talk to the police in the morning. I would like to be left alone now. I really need time to think."

"Of course," the nurse said with a slight smile of understanding. "I have some medication for you. It will help you sleep."

Lora took the medication then watched the nurse as she turned and left the room. Once the nurse was gone, Lora shut off the light next to her bed. In the darkness of the room she could think, she could recall the past few months and how she had met Jeff.

Lora was standing alone next to the fireplace in the family room of her friend's home. The room was filled with people, some she knew and some she didn't know. She was holding a drink in her hand and hoping no one would notice her. Lora glanced up in time to see Jeff come into the room. He stood tall and proud. He had dark hair and a pleasant looking face. He was wearing neatly pressed kaki pants, a light blue shirt, a dark blue blazer and no tie. Lora found him to be very handsome. His presence seemed to fill the room.

She watched him as he looked around the room as if looking for someone. When his eyes met hers, he stopped. A pleasant smile came over his face. She was so embarrassed that she looked down at the glass she held in her hands to avoid eye contact with him. When she finally looked back up, she could see him still looking at her. The way he looked at her made her feel uncomfortable. It was almost as if he could see into her soul and knew what she was thinking.

Slowly, he began to work his way across the crowded room toward her. She watched him as he would stop briefly to say something to this person and then to that one. He seemed to know everyone in the room. After each encounter, he would look at her and start moving toward her again. Before long he was standing in front of her.

"Hi. I don't believe we have ever met," he said in a soft disarming voice.

"No, I don't believe we have," she replied with a shy smile.

"My name is Jeff Bowman. Who might you be?"

"I might be Lora Winters," she responded with a slight giggle.

"Aaah, a woman with a sense of humor. I like that."

Lora simply smiled, but did not respond to his comment.

"Can I get you something? A drink, perhaps?"

"No, thank you. I have a drink," she replied as she held up her glass for him to see.

"Would you mind if I get myself a drink?"

"No, not at all."

"I'll be right back."

Lora watched him as he turned and walked toward the dining room where a small bar had been set up. She was watching him so closely she didn't see her friend, Marsha, walked up beside her.

"Pretty sexy, isn't he?" Marsha said startling Lora.

"Damn, Marsha. You scared the hell out of me."

"Well. What do you think of him?"

"Oh, he seems charming enough, I guess. He is good looking," she admitted as she turned back to look at Marsha.

"He's also single and available."

"I'm not sure I'm interested," Lora said with a sheepish smile.

"There isn't a woman in this room who wouldn't jump at the chance to have a date with him."

"We'll see. He has to ask me first."

"You mean you wouldn't ask him for a date?"

"No. I wouldn't."

"Come on, girl, you're a modern woman. Act like it."

"I don't care. I like a man to ask me for a date. I'm a little old fashion that way," Lora said with a smile.

"There's little hope for you," Marsha said shaking her head, then turned and walked away.

Lora wondered if Marsha might be right. Times had changed. It was no longer considered improper for a woman to ask a man out on a date. It seemed to be a time when women asked for what they wanted. To Lora, it still didn't seem right. It wasn't that she was playing hard to get or she didn't approve of a woman asking a man out. It was just the way she liked it. She still liked her men to be gentlemen, to open doors, get drinks, and to ask for dates.

"Is there something wrong?" Jeff asked as he walked up beside her.

Lora had been so deep in thought she had not seen him come back.

"No," she replied feeling a little embarrassed.

"A woman of mystery. How interesting."

Lora smiled at his comment. She had not tried to be mysterious, but it was kind of nice he thought she was.

"Would you like to get out of here?" Jeff asked.

She looked around the room, then looked into his eyes for a second before answering. She could see no reason not to leave with him. After all, he was the only interesting person at the party.

"Sure," she agreed after a moment's hesitation.

They set their glasses on a nearby table and left the party. He had been the perfect gentleman the entire evening.

Over the next several weeks, they began to see each other on a fairly regular basis.

After a couple of months, they were seeing each other almost every day.

As Lora thought about the past few months from the quiet of her hospital bed, she remembered Jeff started working late more and more during the past couple of weeks. Lora had not thought anything about him working so late as he seemed to be a struggling young attorney trying to get ahead. Since Jeff had proposed to her, it was easy to understand why he was working so hard. It wasn't until she barged in on him and his secretary that she really understood what he had been doing on those late nights at the office. She wondered if she would ever be able to trust anyone again.

Her thoughts turned to Mark. He had literally come into her life at just the right time, but it was by accident, literally. She remembered what one of her friends had told her several years ago. "Nothing happens by accident".

Lora shook her head as she tried to reject that theory. Things happened all the time with no logical reason or explanation, she thought. Logic and common sense told her

Mark just happened to be out checking his drive with his dog. There was no other logical reason for him to be out on a stormy night. If her friend was right, there would have to have been some cosmic force, or some supernatural power that put Mark at the very spot she was at, and at just the right time in order for him to save her.

She smiled to herself as the thought about how romantic that sounded, yet how ridiculous the whole idea really was. There were no super natural forces at work here she tried to tell herself. She did have to admit there were a large number of things that had to happen in just the right order and at just the right time for her to meet Mark, especially considering the way she met him, but it was still by accident.

Lora tried to go to sleep, but she was feeling rather uncomfortable. When she closed her eyes and the sight of Jeff and his secretary came to mind, it reminded her that Jeff had been cheating on her and how much he had hurt her.

But far deeper was the damage he had done to her trust in men. She wondered if she would ever be able to trust any man again.

The one thing she knew for sure was she would never trust Jeff again. She didn't even want to see him again, ever.

She no more than thought it when she realized that never seeing Jeff again was not going to happen. She would eventually have to see him to tell him it was over between them.

Gradually, Lora began to feel the effects of the medication and the long hours of the day. The pain and the emotions of the day had drained her of what little energy she had left. She could no longer keep her eyes open and she soon drifted off to sleep.

CHAPTER FIVE

Over the next couple of days, Mark spent a considerable amount of time thinking about Lora Winters. She occupied his thoughts no matter what he was doing. The questions that continued to haunt him were not getting answered, and that caused him some frustration even though he knew it was really none of his business. He tried to do his work, but he found it almost impossible to concentrate. It seemed the harder he tried to forget her, the more he thought of her.

Although Lora had told him that he could come and see her again, he had gotten the impression she really didn't want to see him again. It was this feeling that had kept him from returning to the hospital to visit her.

It was the third day after he had found her that Mark found himself standing on the edge of the road to his ranch house watching a big wrecker pull the remains of Lora's car up out of the canyon. Seeing what was left of the car close up for the second time caused him to remember how lucky she was to be alive.

As he watched the remains of the car being loaded onto a truck, he decided he would go into the city for a few things. While he was in town, he would make a brief stop at the hospital and see how she was getting along. He reasoned that if he had something else to do besides visit Lora, it would not be a wasted trip if it turned out she didn't want to see him. It also gave him an excuse for being in the city.

As soon as the truck left with Lora's car, Mark walked back to his ranch house and prepared a list of some of the things he might like to get while he was in the city. On the list, he wrote the words "Flowers" and "Card". He thought she might like something to brighten her room, even if it was just a little something.

As soon as he was ready, he started for the city. The drive was not all that long, but Mark found himself thinking about Lora all the way there. It was easy for him to remember how bad she looked when he found her. He could also remember how it felt when he picked her up in his arms, and she laid her head on his shoulder as he carried her to the ranch house.

Before he realized it, he was at the hospital. He parked his truck and went directly to the hospital's gift shop where he picked out a nice conservative get well card that he simply signed, "Mark". He also picked out a small cut glass vase with a single yellow rose in it. It was simple, yet elegant. If he remembered correctly, he had read somewhere that a yellow rose meant friendship.

After paying for the flower and the card, he walked down the hall to the elevators. He pressed the call button and waited for the elevator.

While he was waiting, he looked around the lobby. He saw the same man that had run into him in the elevator sitting near a window. The man looked like he might be angry about something. The fact Mark had seen him three days ago in this same hospital caused him to wonder if he was still there after three days, or if he had returned for a visit. Either way, the person he had come to see must really be sick, maybe even close to death. That thought caused Mark to think that he might have jumped to a conclusion about the man being rude. It may have been a simple case where the man had too much on his mind to think about what he was doing. Having someone you care about in the hospital can do that to some people.

Just then the bell rang and the door to the elevator opened. Mark stepped in and pressed the button for the third floor. As the elevator move upward, Mark began to wonder if he was doing the right thing. Lora had not asked him to come and see her again. However, she had not told him to stay away, either.

As the elevator door opened, Mark thought he might be making a mistake. He wondered if he should really be visiting her again. After all, she did have a boyfriend.

He stepped off the elevator and just stood there looking at the nurse's station as the elevator doors closed behind him. Slowly, he turned and looked down the hall toward Lora's room, still not sure if he should visit her.

"Hi," a voice said from behind him.

Mark quickly turned around and saw Lora sitting in a wheelchair. There was an orderly pushing her toward him. She was smiling up at him as the orderly stopped.

"Hi," Mark replied, a little lost for words.

Mark stood there looking down at her. He found it difficult to take his eyes off her. The last time he had seen her, her eyes were red from crying, and she had seemed very depressed. Now she looked much better, more alive. She had good color in her face and a pleasant smile. It wasn't until Mark realized she was looking at the flower that he remembered he had brought it for her.

"Oh, this is for you," he said as he held out the vase.

"Thank you, it's very pretty," she said with a smile. "Would you like to come to my room where we can talk?"

Mark looked up at the orderly as if asking him if it would be all right. The orderly smiled and nodded to indicate it would be fine.

"Sure," Mark replied, as he looked back down at Lora.

"You can take her from here, if you like," the orderly said with a smile.

"Okay."

Mark watched as the orderly turned and walked away. He stepped around behind the wheelchair.

"Oh, this is for you, too," he said as he handed the card to her over her shoulder.

As soon as she took the card, Mark started pushing Lora down the hall toward her room while Lora opened the envelope. She took the card out and carefully read it. She thought about how nice it was that Mark would think about getting her a get well card. After all, he hardly knew her.

When they reached her room, Mark turned, opened the door and pushed her into the room. He stopped suddenly when he saw the large bouquet of bright red roses on the table next to her bed. There must have been two dozen beautiful flowers in the large arrangement. It made his single yellow rose look kind of insignificant, even a little cheap, he thought.

"Push me to my bed, please," Lora said, her voice having a hint of sharpness to it.

Mark looked down at Lora. Although her request had been polite, the sound of her voice indicated she was angry about something, but Mark did as she requested.

As soon as she was close to her bed, she reached out and pressed the button to summon a nurse. Mark thought that she might be experiencing some pain and he became concerned, but said nothing. Within a minute or so, a nurse came into the room.

"You want to get back in bed?" the nurse asked politely as she walked toward Lora.

"No. I want those flowers taken out of here," she insisted.

Mark wondered what was going on. It was a beautiful bouquet and probably very expensive. He could see no reason for her to have them removed.

"Are you sure?" the nurse asked, surprised at her request.

"Yes," Lora insisted rather sharply.

Mark stood silently behind Lora's wheelchair as he watched the nurse walk around to the other side of the bed, pick up the large bouquet of flowers and take them out of the room.

Mark had to wonder what was going on. Why had those red roses upset her so? He wanted to ask her, but he felt he did not know her well enough to ask her what might be a very personal question. Besides, it was none of his business.

"I'm sorry," Lora said looking up at Mark and seeing the puzzled look on his face. "Would you like to sit down for awhile?"

"Ah - - yeah, sure," he replied, not really sure of what he should do.

Mark turned her wheelchair so it was beside her bed. He then walked around in front of her and sat down in a chair. Mark looked at her as she sat there holding the small vase with a single yellow rose in her hands. She seemed to be admiring it.

"Are you all right?" Mark asked, still a little confused.

Lora looked up at him. She could see the concerned look in his eyes.

"Yes," she replied softly.

Lora looked back at the rose Mark had given her. She then looked up at him again.

"Would you mind setting this on my night stand?" she asked as she held out the vase.

"Not at all."

Mark stood up and took the vase from her. He set the vase on the nightstand where the large bouquet had been.

"Thank you," she said with a smile.

"How are you getting along," Mark asked, not really sure what he should say or how much he dared ask her.

"I'm doing pretty well, I guess. I was just coming back from a couple of tests when I saw you get off the elevator."

"Oh," Mark replied.

"It was nice of you to bring me a flower. It really is pretty. And thank you for the nice card."

"You're welcome. I just thought it might brighten your day a little."

"It does," she said with a smile.

Mark was a little uncomfortable sitting in her room with her. Her reaction to the large bouquet of flowers continued to haunt his thoughts. He still couldn't figure out why she had been so upset over them. He couldn't keep from asking her any longer.

"If you don't mind my asking, why did you have the bouquet of roses taken out of your room?"

Lora turned her face away and looked toward the window. She took a deep breath, then let out a long sigh.

"I'm sorry, it's none of my business," Mark said hoping that he had not caused her any displeasure, but knowing he had.

"It's all right," Lora said as she slowly turned back and looked at Mark. "They are from someone I would rather not see again."

"Oh," Mark replied and decided not to say any more about it.

There was a long period of silence between them. Each of them knowing they needed to change the subject, but not really knowing what to say. Mark didn't want to cause her any pain or discomfort, and Lora didn't want to have to explain anything more to him. It left them with little more to say at the moment.

"How are things up on the mountain?" Lora asked.

"They're fine. They pulled your car out of the canyon this morning."

"I never got to see it."

"I doubt you would want to. I'm afraid there isn't much left of it."

"Probably not," she conceded with a long sigh.

"Do you mind if I asked you what happened?   Do you remember what happened?"

"Yes. I remember, but I would prefer not to talk about it right now, if you don't mind. Maybe some other time."

"No, that's fine," Mark said wishing he had not brought up the subject.

Lora sat looking at Mark. She wanted to tell him what had happened, but she was reluctant to say too much. First of all, it was embarrassing to her.

Secondly, she liked him, but she was still hurting from her relationship with Jeff. She had no desire to get hurt again. She also did not want to spill her problems out to someone who was almost a stranger.

Mark looked around the room for a moment or two, then looked back at Lora. She looked a little uncomfortable to him. Maybe it is time for me to go, he thought.

"I guess I had better go and let you get some rest," Mark said as he stood up.

"Do you have to?" she asked, surprised and a little disappointed he wanted to go so soon.

"Yes, I really need to go. I have some errands to run before I go home."

"Oh," she replied as she looked up at him. "Thank you for the rose and the card."

"You're welcome. Do you need anything before I go?"

"No, I don't think so. I'll just sit here for a little while."

"Well, I'd better go," Mark said as he smiled down at her before he left her room.

Lora watched Mark as he left. She noticed he didn't stop at the door and look back. He simply walked out as if he was walking out of her life. That thought sent an uncomfortable feeling through her.

Sitting in her wheelchair and looking at the open door, Lora began to wonder if she would ever see him again. She wished Mark had not gone so soon. Lora had been working up the nerve to tell him what had happened to her when he decided to leave. Now she was wishing she had not waited so long. She felt she owed him at least a "thank you" for saving her life.

It was becoming clear to her that she might like Mark. Yet, at the same time she was afraid to even think about getting involved with another man, any man, even though she had no reason to believe Mark was anything like Jeff. She also wondered if Mark would be any different.

The thought that she might never have the chance to find out if Mark was different, caused her to wish even more that she had told him about the accident. Maybe if she had, he would not have left so quickly and she might have gotten to know him better.

Lora let out a sigh, then turned to look at the single yellow rose sitting on her nightstand. It was a pretty rose and it was nice of Mark to think of her. She had to wonder if his attention to her was simply one of curiosity as to how she was getting along, or was there something more behind his visit.

She mentally noted it had taken him three days to come and see her. If it took him so long, she reasoned his only interest in her was in how she was doing. For some unknown reason, that thought seemed to be disheartening.

Lora quickly convinced herself she would probably never see him again. She couldn't help but think it was probably for the best even if something deep inside her wished it wasn't true. She had already tried to convince herself that any relationship with another man would not be in her best interest, but there seemed to be some force deep within her telling her that might not be the case.

It wasn't long before she rang her bell for the nurse. When the nurse arrived, she asked for help to get back into bed. She was tired and wanted to take a bit of a nap.

As Lora lay in her bed, she thought about her life. She had not had much experience with men and what little she had wasn't good. Jeff had been only her second serious relationship. She had loved him and he had hurt her very deeply.

In her first serious relationship, the guy had dropped her for another woman. She had to wonder if men were all alike, like some women professed, or if there was someone out there just for her. Someone who would treat her well and be faithful to her.

Deep down she knew men were as different from each other as women were. Some were nice and pleasant, while others treated people like dirt. Some were abusive and some were not. Some men were womanizers while other men respected women and were loyal. Her only question at the moment was what kind of a man was Mark?

A second question came to mind. Would she ever find out?

Even as tired as Lora was, she found it hard to get any rest. She tried to close her eyes and put Mark out of her mind. It was not easy for her, but after awhile she finally dozed off.

Mark left the hospital and went directly to his truck. He drove to a nearby shopping mall where he picked up the things he needed. Before heading home, he stopped at the grocery store. He then drove back to the mountains.

As he drove, he could picture Lora in the hospital. He wondered what was troubling her so much. Whatever it was, he was sure it had a direct bearing on her accident. He had a desire to help her, but she had not given him even a hint that she wanted his help.

As Mark thought about her, he remembered the large bouquet of roses she had removed from her room. If he had to put money on it, he would bet it must have been her boyfriend with whom she was upset.

There were others who might send her such an expensive flower arrangement, but not likely a bouquet of twenty-four red roses. She must have had an argument with her boyfriend over something, and it was probably serious. The most serious reason for an argument Mark could think of was cheating. If her boyfriend had been cheating on her, even the biggest bouquet of the most expensive roses would probably not help.

If he was right, the thought that her boyfriend had cheated on her made it easier for Mark to accept the fact she did not want to talk to him about it. It was probably embarrassing and certainly painful for her.

By the time Mark got back to his ranch house it was near dinnertime. He unloaded his truck, took care of his horses and fed Casey. After he had dinner and had cleaned up the kitchen, he walked out onto his porch. He sat down on the porch swing with Casey at his feet and looked out over the canyon. Although it was a pretty view, he was not looking at the view tonight. He was engrossed in his thoughts of Lora. He wanted to see her again, but wasn't sure if he should.

Gradually his thoughts turned to thinking about what Lora was going to do once she was released from the hospital. Based on his past experience, getting around with a cast on her ankle and one on her wrist was going to be difficult to say the least. It would be almost impossible for her to use crutches, and anything other than an electric wheelchair would be almost as difficult. He didn't know what she did for a living, but whatever it was she would certainly find it difficult with her limitations.

From what he knew about such injuries, it was going to take her several weeks before she would be able to return to work. Mark began to wonder if she had anyone who could help her. She probably had a good many friends who would be willing to look after her once she was able to leave the hospital, he thought.

Mark was sure Lora had a place in the Denver area to live. If she had been living up here, he would have seen her at least once in a while.

The thought passed through his mind that it would be nice if she did own the ranch house next to his. It would also be nice if she would come up here to recuperate, although he doubted she would. He knew it was not a very practical idea. After all, it would put her miles from Denver, her doctor and any of her friends.

Although it was not a practical idea, he thought if Lora would allow him to help her, he could get her place all cleaned up and ready for her to move in. It offered her fresh clean air and would be quiet. She would be able to get a lot of rest and take some time for her injuries to heal. She might even find it a good place to get her other problems worked out.

Mark's thoughts were suddenly interrupted by the realization he had never been inside her ranch house. In fact, he wasn't even sure it was her place. If it was her ranch house, he had no way of knowing if the house was a suitable place for her to recover. Although he had been over to the house several times when the old man was alive, he had never actually gone inside.

Mark decided that on the off chance it was her house, he would walk over and see if it would work for her. It might have too many steps or have other problems that would not make it a good place to recover.

Mark went back inside and grabbed a lightweight jacket and a flashlight. It would be dark and cool by the time he got back.

When Mark slipped on his jacket, Casey got all excited. Wherever his master was going, he wanted to go along.

"Come on, boy," he said as he opened the door.

Mark let the dog out of the house, then started out across the small pasture toward the woods. It was not a very long walk to the old man's house, but it was a pleasant one.

As Mark walked along the edge of the canyon toward the house, he could glance back over his shoulder and see the clouds gradually change color as the sun slowly set. That, along with the beautiful and colorful sunrises, made living in the mountains west of Denver a pleasure. It crossed his mind that he would like to have Lora up here to enjoy the beauty of the mountains with him.

It was getting close to dark when Mark arrived at the ranch house. There were no lights on in the house and no car in the driveway. The house was fairly small, yet very comfortable looking. It was nothing fancy, but it did have all the necessities for making it a year round home.

Mark walked up to the front door and tried to look in, but the small windows in the door were frosted glass. He glanced around looking for a window he might be able to see through. He found one behind some bushes. He walked around to the window and looked inside.

The house was too dark inside to see anything very clearly. Mark pressed his flashlight up against the window, then leaned up against the window to look in.

The ranch house looked like it was as cozy inside as the outside had suggested. All the furniture was covered with sheets so it was difficult to tell what style the house was done in. However, the way the sheets hung on the sofa and chair that he could see, he got the impression the furniture would probably be comfortable.

There was a large fireplace with a couple of guns hanging above the mantel. On the mantel, Mark could see several pictures, but he could not make out who were in the pictures. There was also an oil lamp for when the power went out in the mountains.

On the wall he could see several western paintings and a good size bookcase with books and pictures in it. It looked like it would be a very pleasant place for Lora to spend time while she recuperated.

The only thing he was not sure about was the bathroom. He wondered if it was large enough for her to get in and out of in a wheelchair. The doors that he could see to the other rooms looked like they were large enough to get her wheelchair through.

Mark shut off his flashlight and turned away from the window. As he walked back toward the fence he had to cross, he stopped and looked back at the house. It occurred to him that Lora might not want to come here to recuperate. It might be too quiet for her, or too far from her friends. If he suggested to her to come here to recuperate, she might get the idea he was trying to control her life, or she might think he was sticking his nose in where it didn't belong. She might want to remain in Denver.

Mark began the walk back to his ranch house with Casey. He began to realize there was little he knew about her, yet she had captured his interest. He had to wonder if it was because she was so mysterious and secretive about herself, or if it was because he had helped her and needed to know she was going to be all right. The one thing he did know was he had a difficult time getting her out of his mind.

It had gotten fairly late by the time Mark got back to his house. After feeding his dog, he went to his desk with the idea of trying to get something done. When he sat down at his desk, he saw the light flashing on his answering machine.

Hoping it was a call from Lora, he pushed the play button and waited to hear the message. The recorded message was loud and clear. He let out a sigh at the sound of the woman's voice.

"Hi, it's me. Pick up if you're home," then there was a short pause. "I guess you're not home. If you get home before ten, would you please call me?" then the message ended.

Mark looked at the answering machine. It was still a little before ten, but he did not feel like calling her at this hour. He cleared the message off the answering machine and sat back in his chair for a couple of minutes.

After taking time to think, he got up and went into the bathroom. He took a warm shower and went to bed. It took him a long time to get to sleep with all that had happened over the past few days. Every time, he started to think about Lora, the message on his answering machine would disturb his thoughts.

CHAPTER SIX

Mark was up early the next morning. It didn't seem to him that he had gotten very much sleep. He dressed, ate his breakfast, then went out to the barn where he kept his two horses. He let them out of the barn and into the paddocks. Once they were out of the way, he cleaned their stalls and put down new straw. He took the horses back into the barn one at a time to brush and comb them. When he was finished, he turned them out into the pasture where they could enjoy the fresh air and green grass.

When he finished caring for his horses, he started back toward the house. As he came out of the trees and around the corner, he saw a car parked next to his truck. It was a fancy new silver gray Lincoln Town Car.

Mark immediately recognized the car and let out a long slow sigh. The car belonged to Barbara Cooper, the daughter of Frank Cooper, a well-known and very expensive Denver attorney. She was the last person Mark was interested in seeing. If he had wanted to talk to her, he would have returned her call this morning.

Mark stood there and looked at her from behind a large bush. He considered stepping back into the woods and waiting until she left, but that didn't seem right. Besides, he knew she could be very persistent if she set her mind to it. It would not surprise him one bit if she sat there until he showed up no matter how long it took.

She had probably already knocked on the door. If he knew her, it was more than once. He also knew that there was nothing in this world that would get her to come out to the barn to see if he was there. She didn't like his horses and didn't want anything to do with them.

In her opinion, they were nothing but dirty beasts that served no useful purpose. The whole idea of dealing with horses was distasteful to her. She didn't like the idea of cleaning stalls, brushing them, feeding them or riding them.

Much to Mark's dislike, he felt it was probably best if he went and talked to her. It was better to get it over with than to let it drag out.

Mark had been going with Barbara for about four years. They had had some great times together, but lately Barbara had been pushing him to marry her. Their relationship had become strained especially after their last date.

On their last date, they had gone to an expensive and well-known restaurant. It was Barbara's idea, of course.

During dinner, Barbara began telling Mark where she wanted to live after they were married, how their loft apartment in fashionable lower downtown Denver should be decorated, and who their friends should be. Mark was getting tired of hearing it over and over again and wanted out of the relationship. Mark had had enough of her trying to tell him how he should live his life.

Hoping to avoid a scene, he leaned close to her and whispered in her ear so that others in the restaurant could not hear. He told her that he had no intentions of moving into Denver, and he had no intentions of living in some overpriced loft in lower downtown. He also told her that he had no intention of getting married to her, or to anyone else, and that was final.

With that said, Mark leaned back in the velvet-covered booth, gritted his teeth and waited for her to blow up at him. He knew from past experience it was not likely to be a pleasant experience, but he felt it was time to have his say and get it over with.

Barbara's eyes narrowed as she glared at him. All of a sudden, she jumped up and threw her napkin down in the middle of the table tipping over a full goblet of wine. She looked down at Mark for a few seconds without saying anything. Then after a few choice words that no lady should say, she stormed out of the fancy downtown Denver restaurant making sure that everyone saw her.

In that short moment, she had managed to make it very clear to everyone around them that she was mad as hell. It actually surprised him that she did not scream at him for five minutes before storming out of the restaurant.

The one thing Mark had decided to make absolutely clear was he was not about to let any woman run his life. It was one thing to be a part of his life and for him to be a part of a woman's life, but it was something entirely different to try to completely change him to fit into her life.

Mark felt as if he was not a part of their relationship. She had been trying to push him into moving off the mountain and live in an area known as Lodo, a part of Denver that was rapidly being built up into fancy loft apartments and condos built in old renovated warehouses in lower downtown. It was fast becoming the "in" place to live.

Other than the fact he never liked having someone telling him how to live, he liked even less people who didn't listen. And she certainly didn't listen.

Mark sat there for several minutes as he thought about Barbara and her temper tantrums. It was not the first time he had seen her pull something like this. As far as he was concerned, it would be the last time she would do it around him.

Mark looked around the room and saw several people looking at him. He could tell by the look on their faces that they were wondering what he had said to upset the woman. There was no doubt they thought he was the one at fault, but Mark didn't care what they thought. He'd had enough of Barbara.

Mark called over the waiter, got the bill, paid it and left the restaurant with no desire to return. Besides, the restaurant was overrated as far as he was concerned. It was too pricey and the food was not all that good.

Although he liked Barbara in some ways, he didn't like the way she made him feel. There was no question Barbara was a beautiful woman. She was tall with a very nice figure. Her blue eyes sparkled with excitement whenever she was getting her way. She liked a good laugh, but could be very snobbish if she didn't happen to like someone. And when she didn't get her way, she could be down right nasty, vengeful, and even vulgar if she was upset enough.

Barbara was from a very wealthy family, which meant nothing to Mark. He had enough money to live the lifestyle he liked and wanted. He had worked hard to get a college education and to get to where he was, and had no desire to change things.

On the other hand, Barbara had been given everything all her life. She was used to getting whatever she wanted and getting her own way. Maybe that was what was wrong with her, he thought.

As he watched Barbara sitting in her car, Mark was sure that she had come here in an effort to get him to come back to her. He quickly decided that now was as good a time as any to remind her that he had ended their relationship at the restaurant. He would try to get the message across one more time that it was over between them. At least if she threw one of her temper tantrums here, there would be no one to see it but him and Casey; and he already knew Casey didn't care for her.

Mark stepped out from behind the bush and started toward her car. As he approached the car, Barbara turned and looked toward him. He noticed her glance at Casey. Even though she had not come right out and said so, it was obvious that she didn't like Casey any better than she liked Mark's horses. Mark felt she might be afraid of Casey since he was a fairly large dog. In her talking about moving into a loft, she had never once mentioned taking Casey with them.

As Mark approached, she opened the car door and stepped out. She was here with a purpose. He could see it on her face. He could also see it by what she wore. She was wearing a very sexy blouse and tight, very tight, jeans that clung to her shapely hips. She almost never wore jeans. She was here to get him back; and if skintight jeans were what he liked, that was what she would wear, for now.

"Hi", she said with a soft sexy tone to her voice and a sweet smile on her face.

"Hi" Mark replied without any noticeable emotion.

"Where have you been? Out walking with that dog of yours?"

"Yes and no," he replied as he reached down and patted Casey on the head affectionately.

"What is that supposed to mean?" she asked, trying hard to keep any hint of anger out of her voice, but not doing very well at it.

"I was out walking with Casey, but I was also taking care of my horses."

"Oh, them" she said, the tone of her voice indicating she wasn't really interested in what he had been doing.

"What brings you up here?" Mark asked as he ignored her response.

"I came up to tell you that I forgive you for what happened at the restaurant the other night. I know you didn't mean to cause a scene."

"But I didn't cause a scene, Barbara. You did."

"But I wouldn't have if you hadn't been so selfish."

"Me! Selfish?" Mark responded with surprise and a slight chuckle.

"Yes," she replied calmly. "You know how much I dislike it here. There's nothing to do but look out at the trees, which is about as much fun as watching grass grow."

"That's the very reason I like it here."

"Well, I forgive you anyway," she said ignoring him. "We are having a party on Friday night at my father's house. I want you to be there no later than six o'clock."

Mark shook his head and looked at her in amazement. He couldn't believe she was so dense. He was having a hard time believing that he had actually liked her at one time.

"You've got to be kidding," he said. "You are kidding, right?"

"No, I'm not kidding. I will be very upset if you are not there on time," she said like a child demanding to get her way.

"Well. Since you put it that way," Mark said putting in a short pause. "I guess you're going to be very upset with me."

"WHAT!" she almost screamed.

"You seem to be having a very hard time understanding what I'm saying. To make it as clear as I can so you will have no trouble understanding me, I'll just say it very slowly and in plain English. I - - will - - not - - be - - there. And since you do not like it here on the mountain, you don't need to come up here again. Is that clear?" the tone of Mark's voice was clear and firm.

Barbara stood there silently looking at him. The expression on her face made it clear she had not expected him to talk to her like that. She could not believe he was telling her to get out of his life. Barbara didn't know what to say. She had never been rejected so firmly and didn't know how to respond. Her feelings ran from embarrassed to confused, to disbelief and would soon turn to anger.

Mark had not intended to hurt her feelings, but she didn't seem to get the message that he didn't want to see her again without being so brutally blunt. He stepped past her and pulled open the door of her Lincoln. Mark held the door as if inviting her to get back in the car.

Almost in a stupor, she walked past him. She never took her eyes off him as she got into the car. She looked up at him as tears began to appear in her eyes. She finally began to understand. Suddenly, her expression turned to one of anger.

"There's another woman," she blurted out angrily.

"No. There is no other woman," Mark said, his frustration with her showing in his voice.

"Yes, there is," she cried.

Frustrated and a little angry, Mark simply pushed the car door shut and stepped back away from the car.

Barbara started the car and then looked at him through the car window for a moment.

"I'll find out who she is," she insisted.

She looked away, shifted the car into gear and stepped on the gas. As she pulled away, the rear tires of the big car slipped in the gravel driveway throwing loose gravel around.

In a matter of seconds the car disappeared down the long drive. Mark was a little concerned that if Barbara didn't take it easy, she could end up in the bottom of one of the canyons.

Mark looked down at the ground near his feet and let out a long sigh. He was not happy about the way Barbara took their breakup, but there was nothing he could do about it now. It was over as far as he was concerned.

After taking one last look down the long driveway, Mark looked at Casey, patted him on the head, then turned and walked toward the front door of the ranch house. Just as he started to open the door, he stopped and again looked down the drive. He had to wonder if it was really over between them. Her last comment seemed to leave it open for debate. Shaking his head, he turned the doorknob and went inside.

Mark walked through the house and out onto the porch. His thoughts turned to Lora. The thought that Lora could have died in the canyon and not been found for days haunted him. The roads in the mountains were narrow and sometimes very dangerous.

He turned away from the view and went back inside. He sat down at his computer and began to write, but he soon found he couldn't concentrate very well. His mind was cluttered with thoughts of Lora and Barbara.

He remembered Barbara's last statement. She had said she would find out who the other woman in his life was. Mark didn't consider Lora the other woman in his life; but the more he thought about it, the more convinced he became that he might like Lora to be the other woman.

Mark began to wonder what Barbara meant by her comment. Was it a threat? Was it her way of telling him that she was not going to let him drop her so easy? Or was it just something that came into her mind and she blurted it out, which seemed to be one of the few things she was good at. Either way, it was over between them as far as he was concerned, and she might as well accept it.

Mark had no way of knowing what Barbara might do. He knew she could be a real pain in the butt if she didn't get her way.

Barbara was as spoiled a woman as he had ever met. At this moment, he could not remember what it was he had seen in her, or what it was that had attracted him to her in the first place.

He once again turned his thoughts to Lora and began to wonder what she was like. There was no doubt he didn't know her very well. The thought of her reaction to the large bouquet of red roses had given him a hint as to one side of her personality.

For some reason that Mark could not understand, the thought of the bouquet brought to mind the man in the lobby of the hospital. He wondered if he could have been the one who sent her the roses. Mark pushed that thought aside.

Mark decided it was time for him to get some work done. He had done his morning chores. There was nothing left for him to do except to get to work on an article he had been working on.

It took him a little while to get into his writing, but as soon as he did everything else was shut out of his mind. He worked well into the afternoon before he sat back and looked at what he had written. It was good and needed only a little editing before it would be ready to send off to the newspaper.

Mark had a late lunch, and then took a short walk with Casey. Before he realized it, he found himself standing near the back of Lora's ranch house looking out over the valley below. He hadn't intended to be there, but he was there just the same. He had no business being on her property, and he had no idea why he had chosen to walk to her house.

Taking his time, he returned to his own ranch. All the way back, he tried to get thoughts of Lora out of his head, but with no results. It was at that point he knew he was going to have to try to see her again. He knew he had things to do, deadlines to meet. He would meet those deadlines before he would go see Lora again.

Mark spent a good deal of the evening editing his story for the newspaper. When he was done, it was pretty late. He e-mailed the article to the newspaper. When that was done, he took a shower and went to bed.

It wasn't long and he was lying in his bed, his hands behind his head as he looked up at the ceiling. Casey was sound asleep at the foot of the bed. He was tired, but he was not sleepy.   Going to sleep was going to be difficult. This had been an interesting day to say the least. He wondered what tomorrow would bring just before he dozed off.

CHAPTER SEVEN

Lora was awakened by the usual daily routine of the hospital. The nurse had come in to take her morning vital signs. It seemed a little ridiculous to wake her for such things, but it was necessary to make sure she was progressing well and that she was ready for the doctor when he made his rounds.

While Lora sat up and waited for the staff to bring her breakfast, her thoughts turned to Mark. She turned her head and looked over at the single yellow rose that sat on the bedside stand.

She took this quiet time to picture Mark in her mind. He was tall and fairly handsome. He had dark brown wavy hair and deep brown eyes that seemed to look into her soul. She liked the way he looked in a cowboy hat. She chuckled to herself as she could not picture him as the type to say, "Howdy, Ma'am". Other than that, he looked strong and able to take care of himself.

One of the things she could vaguely remember was the strength of his arms as he carried her to his ranch house. That thought led her to think about what it would be like to be held in his arms and to be kissed by him. She closed her eyes as she pictured the scene in her mind.

They would be standing on the large porch at his ranch house overlooking the canyon. The sun would be reflecting off the thin high clouds filling the sky with shades of red, orange and purple. He would be holding her in his arms. She would be looking up at him while he was looking into her eyes. She would simply melt into his arms and he would kiss her passionately.

It was a romantic scene right out of one of her romance novel. It was such a romantic picture that she didn't want to let go of it.

She opened her eyes to find herself still in the hospital with casts on her ankle and arm. Lora couldn't help but think how unromantic she must look.

Lora's thoughts changed to what she had been thinking last night. She knew she could dream all she wanted, but nothing was going to change. Of the two romantic relationships she had had in her young life, both of them had turned out bad. Maybe her friend in collage, who had been about as much a man hater as any woman she had known, was right. All men are the same. But deep down, Lora knew that not all men were alike.

She wanted things to change more than anything in her world and she hoped they would. The real question was is Mark really any different than Jeff? She began to realize there was no way for her to know what Mark was like without giving him the chance to show her.

She knew she was feeling very lonely at the moment, and it was probably not the best time to be thinking about a new relationship. There was no doubt in her mind that it would be nice to have some strong arms around her to hold her and let her know everything was going to be all right. Right now there was little for her to look forward to. It would do her no good to dream about being held by someone like Mark. For her, at the moment, she felt it would be like jumping from the frying pan into the fire.

The thought of work crept into Lora's mind. There was no doubt in her mind it would be awhile before she would be able to return to work. Even when she could return to work it was going to be difficult for her to face those she worked with after what had happened. There would be a lot of questions she didn't feel she was ready to answer. And her closest friends would be giving her all kinds of advice she wasn't ready to hear.

Lora closed her eyes again in an effort to shut out what she knew was to be the inevitable questions and inquiries about why she broke it off with Jeff. She tried to daydream about what it might be like to be with Mark in an effort to shut out all thoughts of Jeff from her head. They could go walking in the woods together, but that would have to wait until she was able to walk again. They could spend time in front of his fireplace with a glass of wine and a few pillows to lie on. It all sounded so romantic to her that she could not help but wish for it to happen, but she had wished for that before with less than perfect results.

Suddenly it occurred to her there was a possibility she might not ever see Mark again. He had left her room in the hospital without saying anything definite about coming back to see her. The thought he might not come to see her again made her feel a bit depressed.

It occurred to her that her sharp reaction to the large bouquet of roses might be part of the reason he wouldn't come back. She wished her reaction to them had been different and that she had given him a better explanation of why she had them taken away.

She also knew it was only part of the reason he might not come back to see her. The other part was the fact she had not made it clear to him that she wanted to see him again.

"Oh, well. It's probably better this way," she said out loud to herself.

"What would be better this way?"

Lora's eyes flew open and she turned her head to see one of the nurses coming in with her breakfast tray. She could feel her face get warm and was sure she was blushing.

"Nothing," Lora replied softly.

"Here, let's get you set up a little more," the nurse said as she set the breakfast tray on Lora's bed table.

Lora watched as the nurse took hold of the controls to the bed. She pressed the button that made the head of the bed go up. Once it was high enough, she pushed the bed table up so Lora would be as comfortable as possible while eating.

"Do you need someone to talk to?" the nurse asked, the look in her eyes showing she wanted nothing more than to help.

Lora just looked at the woman. She could see by the look on the nurse's face she was really concerned about her.

"Do I look like I need someone to talk to?" Lora asked softly, her question was a serious one.

"Yes, as a matter of fact you do. I can arrange for one of the psychologists to visit with you, if you like?"

"No, I don't think so. I don't need that kind of help."

"Okay, but remember they are available to you."

"I'll remember," Lora said, then looked at the breakfast on the table in front of her.

Just looking at the breakfast caused her to wonder what Mark was having for breakfast. Her thoughts were disturbed by the nurse saying something to her.

"Oh, by the way, the Sheriff wants to talk to you as soon as you're able. It seems one of our doctors reported that you were assaulted. He reported it last night."

"Assaulted? Why did he do that?" Lora asked sharply.

"I don't know. Maybe it was the disturbance your boyfriend made at the nurse's desk, along with the temper tantrum he threw when he was told you would not see him. The doctor felt he may have beaten you before the accident. It seems the doctor believes that some of your minor injuries are not really consistent with the accident. He wondered if you might have had the accident as a result of your boyfriend assaulting you."

"That sure explains one thing," Lora said thoughtfully.

"What is that?" the nurse asked.

"Why one of the sheriff's deputies questioned the man who found me the way he did. He practically accused him of pushing my car into the canyon. But you said the doctor reported it last night. Mark was questioned the day after the accident. Why didn't the sheriff come and talk to me sooner?"

"I don't know. You'll have to ask them. All I know is they are very interested in knowing what happened to you."

"I'm sure they are," Lora said with a long sigh. "I guess I better talk to them before they start blaming someone for my accident."

"You mean that someone didn't do this to you?" the nurse said with a hint of surprise in her voice.

"What are you saying?" Lora asked.

"Everyone here thought that your boyfriend beat you. We thought that was why you didn't want to see him."

"No, he didn't beat me up."

"I don't understand. How did you get all beat up like this?"

"It's a long story," Lora replied with a sigh.

"Then, why don't you want to see him. He has been here since you were brought in. He is very upset."

"I'll bet," she replied sarcastically as she turned and looked out the window.

"He has been trying to get us to let him see you since shortly after you were admitted."

"He has?" she asked as she turned back and looked at the nurse.

"Yes," the nurse replied with a smile.

"Well, I still don't want to see him."

"Okay," the nurse said as she shook her head and left Lora's room.

It was obvious the nurse didn't understand why Lora didn't want to see her boyfriend. But Lora thought about what the nurse had said. She found it hard to believe Jeff had been there trying to see her for so long. She figured that he would have gotten the message that she didn't want to see him and to leave her alone. Lora was sure he couldn't possibly have anything to say to her that would make up for what he had done. She could tolerate a lot of things from a man, but cheating on her was not one of them.

Lora picked at her breakfast as she thought about what she would tell the sheriff's officer when he came by to see her. She knew that telling them about the accident was not going to be easy. She was also going to tell Jeff that he was no longer welcome in her life. That part would be easy, it was facing him that would be hard.

Lora knew Jeff might be considered the major cause of her accident, but it was really not his fault. Granted, she was upset and emotionally out of control because of what she had found him doing, but she was the one who got in the car. She was the one who raced for the mountains. She should have known enough not to drive so fast when she could not see clearly. Her lack of control of her emotions and her inability to see clearly had almost killed her.

Lora had not eaten very much of her breakfast. She wasn't very hungry. Her mind was filled with what would happen next. She had a lot of things to clear up with the police, with her ex-boyfriend and with Mark.

She remembered what Mark had told her about the Sheriff's deputy who had visited him. He had gotten the impression they were looking at him as a suspect in the cause of her injuries. She could not let that go on. She had to talk to the sheriff's officer as soon as possible before she caused the one person who had gone out of his way to help her any more trouble.

She also knew she had to talk to Mark and explain to him what had happened. It crossed her mind that Mark would probably be upset with her once he found out what had happened, but she had to risk it. He had to know everything even if it meant she would not see him again.

Lora reached over and pressed the call button to summon a nurse. The light above her bed came on, as well as the one outside her door. It took several minutes for a nurse to come to her door.

"What do you need?" the nurse asked as she walked to the side of Lora's bed.

"I would like you to get hold of the sheriff's office as soon as possible. I have to talk to them. I need to straighten out a few things with them before this goes too far."

"There was one here last night, but you were sleeping. He said he would return this morning to talk to you."

"Thank you," she replied as she leaned back and relaxed. "If I'm sleeping when he comes by, make sure you wake me. I need to talk to him."

"Sure. Is there anything else you need?"

"No. Thank you. Not right now."

Lora watched as the nurse turned and left the room. She spent the next while thinking about what had happened. It was time to get it all off her chest. She had always been told by her grandfather that it was best to get things off your chest. It would make you feel better, he always said. She wasn't so sure if it would make her feel better or not, but it had to be done.

She looked over at the bedside table at the single yellow rose. Lying next to the vase was the piece of paper with Mark's phone number on it. She thought about calling him and explaining to him why he had gotten the third degree from the Sheriff's deputy, but decided to wait until after she talked to the sheriff.

As she stared at the phone number, she wondered if he would even talk to her. She also began to wonder if it would be best if she simply let things lie. Once she talked to the sheriff, they would have no reason to bother him again. Maybe she should just forget about Mark and let him forget about her.

Lora tipped her head back against the pillow and closed her eyes. She had caused enough trouble by not talking to the sheriff earlier. Now it was time to straighten things out and let everyone get on with their lives, including herself.

CHAPTER EIGHT

Mark woke with the sun shining in his bedroom window. He turned and looked at the clock next to the bed. It was still very early in the morning, earlier than he would normally get up. He rolled over and thought about going back to sleep, but felt something at the foot of the bed. He sat up and looked. Casey was still sleeping and apparently had no intentions of getting up.

Mark dropped back down on his pillow. As the fog of sleep slowly cleared from his mind, he began to think of Lora. It once again crossed his mind that it would be nice if she would come up here to recuperate, but in reality, it was very unlikely.

He looked over at the morning sunrise and decided he had spent enough time in bed. Mark had things to do and he was not getting them done lying in bed wishing for something that was not going to happen.

After a brief time in the bathroom, he went to the kitchen to get breakfast. After feeding Casey, he made his own breakfast and sat down to eat it. When he was done, he went outside to take care of his horses.

As he cleaned their stalls, he remembered it had been some time since he had ridden either of them. There was nothing he had to do so he decided they needed some exercise and he needed some time to think. Besides, it was as good a time for a ride as any.

He put a bridle and saddle on his favorite horse, then slipped his boot into the stirrup, swung his leg over the horse and sat down in the saddle. After patting his horse on the neck, he reined his horse around and started down along a narrow trail that wound around behind his place, then on around the lower edge of the Winters' ranch and off onto some national forest land where he could ride without crossing anyone's private property.

Casey always liked to go and would run beside Mark and his horse as they trotted along a trail in the woods. It was the kind of morning Mark liked. The air was clear and fresh, and the temperature was cool enough that a light jacket was enough.

After riding out some distance from his ranch, Mark decided that it was time to turn back. He knew it would be a little out of his way to swing around and go past the front of Lora's house, but it would provide a little different scenery. It would also give him a chance to check on the place at the same time.

As Mark came around the curve near Lora's ranch house, he noticed a car in the driveway. It was a black BMW sport sedan. It looked like one of those expensive ones to him, but more importantly he had not seen the car before. He wondered if one of Lora's friends was checking out the place for her. If that was the case, whoever it was might know how Lora was doing.

As he rode closer to the car, he saw a man half hidden by the bushes. The man had his hands cupped up against a window and was peering into the house. He wondered what the guy was doing there.

The man certainly didn't look like a common thief that might be casing the place. He was too well dressed for that. He was wearing what appeared to be a rather expensive suit. Mark decided to find out what the guy was up to.

"Hey," Mark called out. "What do you think you're doing?"

Jeff straightened up and turned around to look at Mark. He started to carefully work his way out from behind the bushes. It was apparent he had no intentions of getting his expensive suit dirty.

As Mark swung out of the saddle, he recognized the man as the one who had been so rude at the hospital. He had to wonder what he was doing here.

"I was just looking over the place," Jeff said, once he was out from behind the bushes.

"Why?"

"I don't think that is any of your business, cowboy," Jeff said with a grin.

Mark didn't like the way he said "cowboy". He got the impression that the way he said it meant he considered cowboys lower in status than himself.

"Well, hotshot," Mark retorted, "Let's find out if the sheriff thinks you're trespassing on private property is none of his business."

"You'd call the Sheriff just because I'm looking in a window?"

"In a heartbeat. We call people like you Peeping Toms around here. We don't have much use for Peeping Toms. Sometimes they end up getting shot for it.

"You'd shoot someone for looking in your window?"

"If it was my window, I sure as hell would."

"But this is not your window, is it?"

"No, it's not. So I guess we'll see what the Sheriff thinks about it," Mark said.

Jeff grinned and sort of snickered as if he didn't believe Mark would call the sheriff.

"You don't recognize me, do you?" Mark asked.

"We've met before?" Jeff replied as he looked at Mark in an effort to remember where he might have seen him.

"Sort of. Let's just say it was a brief encounter."

"I don't remember ever meeting you. Would you mind refreshing my memory?" he asked not sure if this cowboy just might be more important than what he appeared.

"You ran into me in the hospital the other day and almost knocked me down," Mark said.

"Oh, yeah? Oooh, I remember," Jeff said without a hint of an apology.

Mark took an immediate dislike to him. He was arrogant, obviously inconsiderate and down right rude. Mark had overlooked his rudeness at the hospital, but this was different. He was trespassing on private property.

"I don't know what you do for a living, but somewhere along the way you either forgot or you never learned your manners. In this part of the country, at least up here, you don't go snooping around in other people's windows or traipsing around on other people's property. It's called trespassing. Now I suggest you leave before I have the sheriff up here to remove you. I don't think the owner would like you being here very much."

"I suppose now you're going to tell me that you are a friend of the owner?" Jeff asked with a smirk on his face.

"As a matter of fact, yes I am," Mark replied without any hesitation.

Jeff looked at Mark for a minute. It was quickly becoming clear he must know Lora, but then why wouldn't he? He apparently lived around here, probably close by. The more Jeff thought about it, the more he was interested in finding out how well he knew Lora and just what her involvement with him might be.

"How do you know the owner?" Jeff asked.

"I don't think that's any of your business."

"I think it is since I'm going to marry her," Jeff said with a sinister grin.

Mark just looked at him for a minute. He didn't know what to say, but he made every effort not to let it show that it was a surprise to him.

"Does she know that?" he asked casually.

"She certainly does," he said still grinning from ear to ear.

"Are you the one who sent her the two dozen expensive bright red roses?"

"I sure am," he replied, the look on his face showing the world how proud he was of himself, and how surprised that this cowboy knew about it. "How do you know about that?"

"You're the boyfriend?" Mark asked, ignoring his question.

"That's right."

"Well, maybe I shouldn't say anything, but why did she have the roses taken out of her room as soon as she saw them and had the nurse deposit them in the trash so she didn't have to look at them?"

The stupid grin on Jeff's face quickly changed. He looked at Mark as if he didn't know what he was talking about.

"She had them removed from her room as soon as she saw them," Mark added, just to make sure he understood what he had been told.

"You don't know what you're talking about."

"I was there when she first saw them. She had them taken away immediately. She said they reminded her of someone she wanted very much to forget. And if you're her boyfriend like you claim to be, explain to me why she won't let you visit her in the hospital?"

Jeff turned a little pale then quickly straightened his shoulders in an effort to recover. He had to wonder how much he knew about what had happened between Lora and him.

"It's just a little misunderstanding," Jeff declared.

"I think "a little misunderstanding" is a very large understatement. She doesn't want to see you. Doesn't that tell you something?" Mark asked. "Or are you too stupid to get the message?"

"I don't think any of this is your business," Jeff said for a lack of anything else to say that would make any sense.

"Maybe not, but I can assure you I will make it my business if I find out that you were in anyway responsible for her accident," Mark said, the tone of his voice making it clear he meant what he said.

"She had an accident. That's all it was and that is all there is to it," Jeff insisted.

"Maybe, maybe not. Either way, you get out of here before I call the sheriff."

Jeff stood there for a few seconds looking at Mark as if he wasn't quite sure if Mark would carry out his threat. The one thing he did know was that his firm would not like having his name in the paper for breaking the law.

Jeff turned and started for his car. When he got to the car, he opened the door and stood next to it looking at Mark.

"The day is not far away when you will be the one trespassing, and I will have you thrown off."

The expression on Mark's face didn't change. He simply looked at Jeff and waited for him to get into his car. Once Jeff was in the car, Mark stood next to his horse and watched as Jeff drove away.

As soon as Jeff was gone, Mark swung up into the saddle and started for home. He watched the road to make sure Jeff didn't circle around and return.

Once Mark was home, he took care of his horse then went into the house. It was getting on toward noon, so he took a little time to have lunch.

While he was fixing his lunch, he thought about Jeff and Lora. He found it hard to believe Lora would have any kind of interest in such an arrogant, pompous ass. Although he didn't know Lora very well, he felt she was smart, intelligent, and, of course, beautiful.

Jeff was ambitious to a fault, arrogant, self-centered and probably the only person Jeff loved. He was also sure that Jeff could be very charming if he thought it would serve his propose. Mark had to wonder if Lora had finally seen the real Jeff and didn't like what she saw.

Mark had to think about what Jeff had said. He really didn't know either of them very well, but he had met people like Jeff before. It didn't take much to figure out what he was like. It came to mind he was not all that much different from Barbara.

But Lora was a different matter. Mark did not know what kind of a person Lora was. However, he did know she had been hurt and hurt deeply by Jeff. He had betrayed her trust in some way that made it difficult, if not impossible, for Lora to forgive him.

The first thought that crossed Mark's mind was she had caught him with another woman. That seemed like the most obvious cause for her reaction to his flowers and for her not to allow him in her room. Cheating was the type of betrayal that caused a person not to want anything that would remind them of the betrayer.

As Mark sat and ate his lunch, he began to think it might be a good idea to go visit Lora again. She might like to know someone had been by her place and was snooping around. It would also give him a chance to see her again. Maybe this time she would tell him why she had been up on the mountain on such a stormy night.

Mark cleaned up and changed his clothes. He got in his truck and headed for the hospital.

As Mark drove toward the hospital, he began to think about what he was doing. He had to wonder if it was a good idea to visit someone who might have a boyfriend, or might be in the process of ending a relationship. There was really no reason for him to get involved other than to let her know that Jeff had been at her ranch. He had done what he could for her as a Good Samaritan and that was all he had intended to do.

That thought caused Mark to slow down a little and take another look at what he was doing. He had to ask himself if he had any right to stick his nose in where it didn't belong. His answer was a resounding, 'no'.

If things were different, he might consider asking Lora out, but not now. He was sure she needed time to end her relationship, or more correctly put, decide if she really wanted to end it. Mark needed time to make sure his relationship with Barbara was over before he started looking for someone else to share his time.

As he came to the next exit on the interstate, he pulled off and coasted up the ramp. He stopped at the end of the ramp and just looked ahead. His mind was so occupied with thoughts of what he had been thinking about that he didn't notice the police car that had pulled up behind him. It was the quick short blast of the police siren that brought him back to reality.

Mark looked in his rearview mirror, waved and pulled into the intersection as he turned to go across the overpass. The police car turned and was still behind him, but he had not turned on his overhead lights.

When Mark got to the other side of the overpass, he signaled to turn back onto the interstate and moved over into the turn lane. The police car did not follow him. Instead, the police car went on past and disappeared around a curve.

Mark turned onto the entrance ramp to the Interstate and started back toward the mountains. He decided he had made the right choice by turning around and going back home. He quickly convinced himself he didn't need the hassle of getting involved with a woman who was in the middle of ending a somewhat rocky relationship. He had been down that road before and didn't need the problems it would most likely bring him.

As he drove back to his ranch house, Mark tried to put Lora out of his mind. When he finally succeeded, he began to think of Barbara and remembered what she had said before she drove away from his place.

He couldn't help but smile. The thought of Barbara and her demands made him ask himself why he would want to go from one messed up relationship to another. What he needed right now was some peace and quiet for a little while, he thought. He needed some time to get his own head on straight.

When Mark pulled into drive to his ranch house, he noticed a sheriff's car parked in front of his home. He let out a sigh and shook his head in disgust when he saw the same deputy that had questioned him before leaning against the front fender of the patrol car. Mark had to wonder how long he had been waiting for him. He knew it couldn't have been more than a half an hour. Just the look on the deputy's face told Mark that he was sure this was not going to make his day.

Mark pulled up in front of his ranch house, shut off the engine and looked at the deputy. Knowing he was not going to get rid of the deputy until he talked to him, he opened the truck door and got out.

"What do you want now?" he asked as he walked around the front of his truck.

"I just have a few questions for you," the deputy said, his voice sounding casual and relaxed.

"To be perfectly honest with you, I don't think I want to answer any more questions from you. So unless you have a warrant, I might suggest you get in your car and leave my property," Mark said in a calm, controlled voice as he looked the deputy in the eyes.

"That's not being very friendly," the deputy said.

"You know, after the last time you were here, I don't feel very friendly toward you. You came onto my property and accused me of causing, or at the least having something to do with Miss Winters' accident. That doesn't set very well with me. So, if you have questions you need answered, you can either ask my attorney, or you can have the Sheriff, himself, come here to ask me. Good day, deputy," Mark said, then turned and walked toward the front door of his ranch house.

As Mark unlocked the door to his ranch house, he glanced over his shoulder and saw the deputy was standing there watching him. He had no idea what the deputy was thinking, but then he really didn't care. He turned the doorknob, opened the door and went inside.

Not sure what the deputy might do, he moved over next to a window and peeked out to see what the deputy was doing. The deputy just stood there for a minute or two as if he expected Mark to come back outside. When Mark didn't, the deputy got back in his car and sat there.

After a couple of more minutes, he got on his radio and called someone. He must not have been very happy with the reply he got because the deputy had a disgusted look on his face.

Suddenly, the deputy put the car in gear and drove away. Mark wondered who he had talked to, but he didn't really care as long as the deputy was gone. If he had talked to the Sheriff, all the better. At least that way, the Sheriff would know the only way he was going to get Mark to cooperate was to ask the questions himself, or get a warrant issued. Mark doubted that he had grounds to get a warrant.

Mark decided to sit down and have a cup of coffee. He had no more than taken a couple of sips when his phone rang. He got up from the table and walked across the kitchen and picked up the phone next to the sink.

"Hello?"

"Hi, honey," the voice on the other end of the line said.

There was no doubt in Mark's mind who was calling. It was the last person he wanted to hear from even if her voice sounded bubbly and happy.

"Barbara, I thought I made it clear that it is over between us," Mark said as he let out a long sigh of frustration.

"You were just upset. When people are upset they say things they don't really mean. I forgive you."

"I was not upset."

"Yes, you were."

"Fine, I was upset," he said knowing full well that she was not listening to him, and it didn't matter what he said.

"See. Don't you feel better?" she asked, her voice sounding cheerful and light.

Mark didn't respond to her question. He stood there with the phone in his hand shaking his head in disbelief. He couldn't believe he had even liked this woman at one time. He considered simply hanging up on her, but he knew it would just give her reason to call back again.

"What do you want?" he asked rather bluntly.

"I was just calling to remind you of the party at my father's home. I want you to be here no later than six o'clock," she said as if they had never had the earlier conversation.

Mark let out another long sigh. She was not going to give up, he thought.

"Did you hear me?" she asked when he didn't say anything.

"Oh yes. I heard you," he replied. "But I . . ."

"Good," she replied cutting him off. "Love you, dear."

The phone went dead before Mark could tell her that he would not be there. He looked at the phone for a second then hung it up. He was sure she was thinking if she didn't give him a chance to say no, that everything would be okay.

Mark leaned against the kitchen counter as he thought about what had just happened. It was rapidly becoming clear to him that she was not going to let him be. He was going to have to do something to make it clear that it was over between them, and he could think of several ways to get the message to her.

One of the thoughts that passed through his mind was it would serve her right if he could fix her up with Jeff. They would be at each other's throats all the time, he thought with a smile. The disappointing thing was that it wasn't going to happen.

Mark returned to the kitchen table and sat down to finish his coffee. His mind was filled with questions, the main one being how was he going to get it through Barbara's head that it was over between them. The problem was he wanted nothing more to do with her, but didn't want to hurt her, either. The bottom line was that it was looking as if she was giving him no choice. The one thing he did decide was that no matter what happened he would not be going to her party. If that didn't get the message across to her, he didn't know what would.

After Mark finished his coffee, he went into his study and sat down in front of his computer. He started working on his column for next week's newspaper. He began typing on the computer not really sure what he was going to write about. It wasn't long before he was absorbed in what he was writing.

Time passed without Mark giving any thought to anything except the article he was writing. He had been able to shut out everyone and concentrate on his writing. By six o'clock, he had finished the first draft of his article and was pleased with how it had gone.

The article was about what it was like to live up in the foothills above the city of Denver a hundred years ago. Much of what he had written had come from information Wilbur Winters had told him on their many visits. Mark had found Wilbur to be a fountain of information about the history of Colorado, especially in the Denver area.

Although the draft of his article was finished, he knew from experience it was not done. He would have to rewrite it several times to get it just the way it should be. It was now time to let it set for a while. It was how he wrote all of his articles.

Mark leaned back and looked at the computer screen. He took a deep breath before he reached over and turned off the computer. He stood up and went out to the kitchen. Tonight he was going to have soup and salad.

After he finished eating, he put on his cowboy hat and went out to the corral. He spent the next hour or so taking care of his horses. Casey laid in the barn and watched his master as he worked. When Mark was done, he went back to the house with Casey at his side. Casey knew it was time for his master to feed him.

Mark had no more than finished cleaning up the kitchen and feeding Casey when the phone rang. He reluctantly reached over and picked up the phone.

"Hello?"

"Is this Mark Howard?" the female voice on the other end of the line asked.

"Yes," he replied wondering who was calling him.

"This is, ah, Lora Winters."

"Oh, hi. How are you doing?"

"Pretty good, I guess," she replied, her voice showing she was relieved to hear a pleasant voice.

"What can I do for you?"

"I know you have done a lot for me already, but I was wondering if, - - well, maybe I shouldn't ask. I'm sorry to take up your time," she said apologetically.

"No, wait," Mark said, afraid that she was about to hang up before he found out what she wanted. "What is it you need?"

"I really have no right to ask you to help me. You have done so much already."

"It's all right. I gave you my number so you could call me if you needed anything. What is it you need?"

"Well, ah, you will tell me honestly if I'm asking too much of you? Won't you?"

"Yes, of course."

"The doctor said I could be released from the hospital the day after tomorrow, on Friday."

"That's great. So what's the problem? You need a lift home?"

"Well, yes, but I don't really want to go to my town house here in Denver. I would really like to go to my grandfather's ranch in the foothills. It is not very far from where you live. But there's a problem," she said then hesitated.

"What's the problem?"

"It hasn't been used in a long time, and I don't know what condition it's in. I mean, I don't know how much trouble it would be to get it ready to live in."

"Would you like me to go over there and get it ready for you to move into?" he asked.

"Yes, I would. I would be more than happy to pay you for your trouble."

"That won't be necessary. I'd be glad to do it for you, but I have one problem. I don't have a key to get in."

"Oh. Around back on the patio deck there's a flower urn made of cement. Under the urn you will find a key to the back door. You can use it to get in."

"Okay. Is there anything else?"

"No. I've asked more than I have a right to already," she said, her voice showing she was relieved he would help her.

"Okay. I'll see to it that everything is ready for you. Do you want me to come and get you when you're ready?"

"Well, ah, that would be nice, but I can get a cab to take me."

"A cab from the hospital to here can be very expensive. I'll just come and get you if you give me a call when you're ready," Mark said. "But keep in mind it takes me about an hour to get to the hospital from here, maybe a little more."

"I know," she said.

"Give me a call when you're ready," Mark said.

"Okay, and thank you. Thank you so much"

"You're welcome. I'll talk to you later," Mark said, then hung up the phone.

Mark stood there and looked at the phone as he thought about his conversation with Lora. She was going to come up here to recuperate after all. The thought of her coming up on the mountain caused him to have mixed feelings about it.

First of all, what was she really coming up here for? Was it to recuperate, or was it to get away from her boyfriend? Or was it to give herself time to decide what she was going to do about him? In either case, he needed to help her while keeping his distance. He didn't want to be the reason for her making a decision one way or the other. She had to decide what she wanted on her own.

When he had seen her the last time in the hospital, Lora had not told him why she was on the mountain in the first place. She hadn't even told him what happened that caused her to lose control of her car and crash into the canyon.

Mark began to wonder what he was getting himself into. There was no doubt her boyfriend could be a real pain in the ass if he set his mind to it. He could cause a lot of trouble, trouble Mark didn't need.

He began to think he should have left well enough alone. If he had just let things be once she was taken to the hospital, he wouldn't be having these misgivings now.

Mark had to wonder if his troubles with Barbara were a big part of his misgivings. She could be a real pain without half trying.

No matter what might happen, it was too late to change things now. He would keep his commitments. Other than that, he would keep his distance and see how things worked out.

The one thing he did know was it was time to try and get some sleep. He had promised Lora that he would make sure all was ready in her ranch house, and he would do that. After that, he would back off and try to get his own relationship ended before he could think about getting involved with someone else.

Mark went inside and got ready for bed. It wasn't all that late when he finally got into bed, but sleep did not come easily. His mind was too cluttered to let him get to sleep quickly.

CHAPTER NINE

Morning came early to Mark and his small ranch. He was up as the sun was coming over the horizon. He knew he had a lot to do if he was going to get Lora's ranch house ready for her to move in. However, a good breakfast was the first order of business.

After letting Casey out for his morning run and putting his food on the porch, Mark fixed himself some breakfast. While he was eating his breakfast, the phone rang. He got up and walked over to the phone to answer it.

"Hello?"

"Is this Mr. Mark Howard?" the male voice asked.

"Yes. Who is this?"

"This is Sheriff Butler."

"I was wondering if I was going to hear from you."

"I understand you refused to talk to my deputy yesterday. Is that right?"

"Yes, it is. Are you at all interested in why I refused to talk to him?"

"Yes, I am."

"I refused to talk to him because the first time he was here he practically accused me of having something to do with Miss Winters' accident. He had no evidence to support that kind of an attitude. It appeared to me that he was more interested in placing the blame on me than he was in getting to the facts of what happened," Mark explained.

"You think he was blaming you?"

"As a matter of fact, yes."

"I wasn't there so I don't know what he asked you or how he asked it. He had just come from a domestic violence call, and maybe he thought you and Miss Winters might have had a lover's spat."

"Well, he needs to learn how to separate one investigation from another.

"But as I told him, I hadn't even met Miss Winters until that night, after the accident. I had no idea what she was doing on my drive until I found where she had gone off the road on the curve above my place. I had no idea what she was even doing up here at that hour of the night. And I had no idea what her name was until she told me her name while we waited for the helicopter to take her to the hospital. I had no idea where she lived until after I climbed down into the canyon to see if anyone else was in the car, and I retrieved the registration. That about sums it up."

"But you do now?" he asked.

"I do now what?"

"Know where she lives."

"Sort of. She has a town house in Denver. I don't remember the address. I also figured out that she is the granddaughter of the old man who lived just up the road from me."

"I see. Would you mind if I stop by and visit with you a little later this morning, say about ten o'clock?"

"Not at all, Sheriff, but I won't be here. I will be at Miss Winters's place. It's the next drive up the road from mine. You can talk to me there, if you wish."

"I thought you said you didn't know her?"

"I didn't know her until the night of the accident. I'm just going over to get her place ready for her. She is coming up here to recuperate. I'm just being a good neighbor."

"I see," he said, his voice indicating he wasn't sure Mark was telling him the whole truth.

Mark had heard that kind of response before. He knew the Sheriff wanted to know just what Mark's relationship with Lora's was, but wasn't ready to come right out and ask.

"I'll talk to you about ten," the Sheriff said.

"Right," Mark replied, and then hung up the phone.

Mark looked at the phone for a moment after hanging it up. He shook his head in amazement, then sat back down to finish his breakfast. When he was finished, he took his hat off the rack next to the door and stepped outside. Looking up at the sky, he thought it was going to be a rather nice day. The sky was clear and there was almost no breeze.

Mark went to his barn and let the horses out into the pasture. As soon as he was done taking care of their stalls, he started walking off across the field toward Lora's ranch house with Casey alongside him.

As he walked across the field, he began to wonder how Lora was going to get along in her ranch house. It crossed his mind she must have thought that out or she wouldn't come up here.

When Mark got to the house, he stepped up on the rear patio deck. Sitting on the corner of the patio was a gray cement urn just like Lora said there would be. Whatever had been growing in the urn had died a long time ago as there was nothing left but dried vines in it.

He walked over to the urn and looked around before he knelt down next to it. He tipped the urn forward with one hand while he reached around behind the urn with the other. His finger touched a key right where Lora had said it would be. He picked up the key and set the urn back.

Mark walked over to the back door, slipped the key into the lock and unlocked the door. He opened the door and went inside. The back door entered into a laundry area just off the kitchen. After a brief look around the laundry area, Mark stepped into the kitchen and looked around. The kitchen was neat and orderly. The table sat in the middle of the room and had a thin coat of dust on it, but otherwise the place seemed clean.

After a brief walk through the house, Mark had a good idea of what needed to be done. Since the refrigerator had been cleaned and left open, the only thing he needed to do was to wipe it out and turn it on.

Mark immediately went to work cleaning the house. He uncovered the furniture and the table lamps. The sheets he took outside to shake the dust off before stacking them neatly on the washing machine. It didn't take him long to find the vacuum cleaner. He vacuumed the entire house and then started cleaning the bathroom.

He was just about done with cleaning the tub when he heard Casey bark a couple of times, then he thought he heard a car door shut. Mark was sure it was the Sheriff. He wasn't all that anxious to talk to the Sheriff, but he had said he would. Mark started for the front door.

As he walked by the window, he noticed a black BMW parked in front. He knew Jeff had come back. He let out a sigh as he walked to the door.

Approaching the door, he could hear Jeff trying to get the door open. It sounded almost as if he was trying to jimmy the lock and break in. Mark reached for the doorknob and jerked open the door, surprising Jeff.

"We're into breaking and entering now, I see. That should look good on your résumé," Mark said as he looked at Jeff.

Jeff was obviously surprised to see Mark inside the house. It took Jeff a minute to recover.

"What are you doing here?" was all Jeff could manage to get out of his mouth.

"I'm not breaking in," Mark replied as he reached in his pocket, retrieved the key and held it up for Jeff to see.

"Where'd you get that?"

"That is none of your business," Mark said as he looked at his watch. "Your timing is almost perfect. The Sheriff should be here in a few minutes. I think he might want to know why you where attempting to break into someone's house."

"Very funny," Jeff said sarcastically.

"You won't think it so funny if you are still here when he gets here."

"You've got no business being in Lora's house. Now get out before I have you arrested."

"That's pretty good. Are you going to use it as part of your defense for breaking in?

Just for your information, the Sheriff is on his way and he knows I'm going to be here."

"I don't believe you. Now get out of my way," Jeff said as he stepped closer, expecting Mark to move aside.

Mark stood his ground and didn't move. He hoped Jeff would get pushy and lay a hand on him. It would give him a good reason to punch the arrogant ass in the nose and then have him arrested for assault, too.

"I said to get out of the way," Jeff demanded.

"You get off Miss Winters's property or I will have you arrested. I doubt your law firm would like to see your picture in the paper for breaking and entering property that doesn't belong to you," Mark said.

Jeff just stood there and looked at Mark for a moment. He knew Mark was right about his law firm not liking it, but at the moment he didn't care. He didn't like this "cowboy" telling him what to do.

Just as Jeff was about to say something, he heard a car pull into the circle drive in front of the house. Jeff turned to see who else was coming. His eyes got big and his mouth fell open when he saw not one, but two Sheriff's patrol cars pull up behind his BMW.

He turned and looked back at Mark. Mark was smiling back at him.

"I told you so."

Jeff turned back around and watched as the Sheriff got out of one car.

"Which one of you is Mark Howard?" the Sheriff asked as he came around the front of his car.

"I am," Mark replied.

"Who are you?" the Sheriff asked of Jeff.

"Jeffrey Bowman," he replied without offering any additional information.

"What are you doing here?"

"He was trying to break in, Sheriff," Mark said casually.

The Sheriff looked at Mark, then turned and looked back at Jeff.

"Well, Mr. Bowman, why would you want to break into Miss Winters's home?"

"I . . I wasn't . . ah . . breaking in," he replied nervously.

"Sheriff, what would you call it if a man tries to get into a house that is owned by someone else, and he neither has a key for the property or the permission of the owner?" Mark asked.

"Well, if he actually got into the house, it would be breaking and entering. Did he get into the house, Mr. Howard?"

"No. I wouldn't let him in."

"Then it's just breaking. Why are you here, Mr. Bowman?"

"I don't think I will answer that question?"

"Oh. Well, for your information, I already know who you are. You are a lawyer that works for your daddy's big law firm in Denver, which, by the way makes no difference to me. You're the ex-boyfriend of Lora Winters," the Sheriff said as he looked into Jeff's eyes for some kind of reaction.

Jeff didn't know what to say. He had no idea how much the Sheriff knew about him and about his relationship with Lora.

"Is there some reason that you're here? Is there something in the house that belongs to you that you want back, Mr. Bowman?" the Sheriff asked.

"No," he replied nervously.

"Then there is no reason for you to be here. Is that correct?"

"I guess. But what about him?" he asked as he pointed a finger at Mark.

"Mr. Howard is here at Miss Winters's request. He has every right to be here," the Sheriff explained. "You, on the other hand, have no right to be here at all. I would suggest you leave before this goes any further. Do I make myself clear?"

Jeff looked from the Sheriff to Mark and then back at the Sheriff. He wanted to have Mark removed from the property, but he had no idea as to how he could accomplish it without getting himself into trouble with the Sheriff.

"Yes," he replied reluctantly.

"And I might suggest you stay away from here unless Miss Winters personally invites you. Is that also clear?"

"Yes."

"Make sure it is."

Jeff then turned and walked toward his car. As he opened the driver's side door, he looked over the car and glared at Mark. He was mad as hell and he would be back after the Sheriff left. He would deal with Mark in the kind of terms Mark would understand, he thought to himself.

Mark saw the look in Jeff's eyes. He knew it was not going to be the end of it. He had run into men like Jeff before. The kind of men who could not let go of something he felt belonged to him, even when it didn't. It was clear from what the Sheriff had said that Lora was finished with Jeff. It was also clear Jeff didn't like it.

The Sheriff and his deputy watched as Jeff took off. He gunned his car so hard the wheels spun and spit gravel out behind them. As soon as he was gone, the Sheriff turned around and looked back at Mark.

"Well, that takes care of him," he said with a sigh.

"I wouldn't count on it," Mark said as he watched the black BMW disappear from sight.

"Well, we'll see. I would like to have a talk with you, Mr. Howard," the Sheriff said.

Mark looked at the Sheriff then said, "Sure. How about we sit out on the patio out back?"

"Okay."

Mark led the two officers around to the back patio and offered them a seat. After they had all sat down, the Sheriff began to ask his questions.

"What can you tell me about the accident?"

Mark spent the next fifteen minutes telling the Sheriff everything he knew about what had happened that night from the time he found Lora until she was taken to the hospital by helicopter. He also told him about what he had found after Lora had gone.

It became clear to the Sheriff that Mark had nothing to do with Lora's accident. The Sheriff told Mark about what led up to the accident and that Lora had explained that Mark had nothing to do with it.

"So you knew all the time I didn't have anything to do with the accident," Mark said.

"Not really. We didn't find out until a couple of days after the accident. Miss Winters was unable to explain things to us until she was feeling better.

"I guess this guy, Bowman was her boyfriend?"

"He was from the sounds of things," the Sheriff said.

"I get the impression Bowman has a hard time letting go of what he thinks is his, don't you think?"

"It appears so," the Sheriff agreed.

"I just hope I don't have any trouble with him."

"I hope you don't either, but if you should I expect you to call me. I don't want you taking matters into your own hands," the Sheriff said firmly.

"That will be up to him," Mark said as he looked the Sheriff in the eyes.

"I hope he doesn't come around, but he might. I have recommended Miss Winters get a restraining order against Mr. Bowman to keep him away from her and off her property."

"What did she say about that?" Mark asked.

"She said she would think about it."

"In other words, she hasn't done anything to legally keep him away from her. Is that right?" Mark asked.

"That's right, but she can always call us if he trespasses on her property. You can do the same if he comes onto your property. I doubt his firm would like it very much if he is arrested for trespassing," the Sheriff said.

"I can assure you that I will not hesitate one second to file charges against him if he comes onto my property, and I'll make sure it becomes public knowledge."

"Good. Well, I guess I best go and let you get on with your work. By the way, do you know how Miss Winters plans to get here?"

"Yes. I told her I would pick her up and bring her here tomorrow."

The Sheriff nodded that he understood and then turned to leave. Mark stood up and followed the Sheriff around to the front of the house. Mark stood there for a minute with Casey at his side. He had to wonder what would happen next as he watched Sheriff Butler and his deputy drive off.

Mark couldn't help thinking about Jeff. He was hoping he would not have any trouble with Jeff, but he believed he had not heard the last of him.

As soon as the Sheriff had disappeared, Mark took a quick look around and then went back inside the house. He returned to the bathroom to finish what he had started. After completing the cleaning of the bathroom, he continued cleaning the rest of the house and getting it ready for Lora to occupy. He had stopped only long enough to grab a bite to eat for lunch.

When Mark was finished cleaning the ranch house and it was ready for Lora to live in, he locked the house and put the key in his pocket. He returned to his own ranch house with Casey. It was close to six by the time he got home and he was ready to get himself something to eat.

He had no more than walked in the door when the telephone began to ring. Mark hesitated for a moment wondering if he should answer it or just let it ring. It was difficult for Mark to let a phone ring without answering it. He reluctantly picked up the receiver.

"Hello?"

"Hi, Honey. I'm just calling you to find out where you've been. I've been trying to get hold of you all day."

"I've been busy. Listen, Barbara, I'm really tired. It has been a long day and I don't feel like talking right now."

"That's no way to be. I've been wanting to tell you what I would like you to wear tomorrow evening to the party," she said in a little girl sing-song voice she used in order to get her way.

"You never have been one to listen, have you?" Mark said with a note of frustration in his voice.

"I don't know what you mean. I listen to you all the time."

"If you listen to me all the time, then why is it you don't seem to have gotten the message that we are no longer "an item", as you like to put it?"

"When I said you were upset, you agreed with me."

"Yes I did. And I was upset. But you also didn't listen to me when I said I would not be coming to your party," Mark reminded her.

"I didn't think you really meant it."

"That's what I mean. You only hear what you want to hear."

"That's not true," she retorted.

"It is true. I told you it was over between us, and that is what I meant. If you don't want to be embarrassed by my not showing up for your party, you best find someone else to be there with you, or cancel the damn party."

"But the party is for you," she said sadly.

"No. It isn't for me. It was never for me. It is for you. I was the excuse you used so you could have a party. I never wanted the party and I certainly didn't ask for it."

"You really meant it when you said it was over between us, didn't you?" she asked as if it had just soaked into her head.

"Finally, you're beginning to understand. Yes, I really meant it."

"You'll wish you hadn't done this to me," she yelled into the phone.

Suddenly the phone went dead. She had hung up on him, but he wasn't surprised. It was what he had expected her to do. It was her way of dealing with things she didn't like. What surprised him was he was actually getting used to her getting angry and upset when she didn't get her way. For the first time he began to think she finally got the message that it was over. Maybe now she could look for someone who would be more what she wanted in a man, someone who liked the same things she liked and would put up with her temper and her telling him what to do.

Mark set the receiver back down. He was almost relieved that she seemed to finally understand it was over. He could go about his own business. The only thing that disturbed him was her last comment.

Just as he started to leave the kitchen, the phone began to ring again. Mark shook his head in disgust and thought about not answering it. Instead he turned around and grabbed up the receiver.

"I told you that I will not be coming to your damn party," he blurted out into the phone before anything could be said.

"I'm sorry," a soft-spoken female voice said.

"Excuse me?" Mark asked, realizing it was not Barbara.

"Is this Mark Howard?"

"Yes. Who is this?"

"Lora Winters," she replied.

"Oh," Mark said feeling embarrassed. "I'm sorry. I thought it was someone else."

"I sure hope so because I didn't know I was having a party."

They both laughed. Mark was glad Lora was taking it with a sense of humor.

"I'm really sorry. I didn't mean to yell at you."

"That's okay. I guess I got you at a bad time."

"No, it's okay. What can I do for you?" he asked.

"I was wondering about my house."

"Oh. It's all cleaned up and ready for you to move in. I haven't gotten any food yet, but I can get that tomorrow."

"I feel like I'm imposing on you. Are you sure you don't mind helping me?" she asked.

"Don't feel that way. I'm glad to help. We're neighbors."

"Well, I was wondering if you could come in and pick me up around noon tomorrow? The doctor said I could go home by noon."

"Sure, that would be good. Do you think you would feel like stopping off somewhere for lunch?"

"I think so. Anything would be better than the food served in the hospital," she replied, there was a hint of pleasure in her voice at his suggestion.

"You won't be too tired, will you?"

"No, I don't think so. I feel fine. It's just that getting around is a little difficult for me right now."

"No problem. If you feel up to it we can stop at the grocery store and pick up a few things at the same time," Mark suggested.

"That would be great. I'll be waiting for you."

"Good. See you tomorrow about noon."

"Great," she replied then hung up.

Mark hung up the phone and then stood there for a couple of minutes thinking about the call. He was glad that she had accepted his offer for lunch. It pleased him that she seemed to be in better spirits today.

CHAPTER TEN

Mark fixed Casey his dinner and set it outside by the door. He then fixed his own dinner. After dinner, he grabbed his hat and went out to the barn to take care of the horses. It took him less than an hour to take care of both of his horses and get them bedded down for the night.

It had been a long day, but Mark still had some work to do. He returned to the house, turned on his computer and began to rework his article for the newspaper. Casey was lying beside Mark, sleeping.

Suddenly Casey's head came up, as did his ears. Mark looked at Casey and wondered what had caused him to become so alert so quickly.

"What is it, Casey?"

Casey glanced up at Mark, but quickly looked back toward the window and barked once. Mark glanced over at the window. It took him a second before he noticed there were flickering lights coming from the direction of the barn. He quickly realized his barn was on fire.

Mark grabbed the phone next to his computer and called 911. He quickly told the operator that he had a barn on fire. He gave her the location, then hung up the phone.

Both Mark and Casey ran out of the house toward the barn. As they came around the corner, it was clear that the barn was burning pretty well. Mark ran inside with Casey on his heels and opened the stalls to his horses. The horses were reluctant to leave, but a few nips on their heels from Casey got them moving.

While Casey chased the horses out into the pasture, Mark grabbed up the hose and turned on the water. It was just a garden hose, but it was all he had. If he couldn't do anything else, maybe he could keep it from spreading to the buildings nearby. He did his best to water down the buildings closest to the barn.

It wasn't long before he heard the sounds of sirens, but he knew it was too late to save the barn. The best he could hope for was to keep it from spreading to his workshop and the storage building where he stored hay, feed and his tack for the horses.

It took the fire department over an hour before they had the fire under control and another hour to get it completely out. Mark had felt so helpless standing there as the local firemen worked hard to save what they could. It turned out that the barn was a total loss, but he had managed to save his two horses. The firemen had managed to save Mark's workshop and storage building.

"You got any idea as to how it started?" the Fire Chief asked as he walked up to Mark.

"No. I was hoping you could tell me," Mark replied.

"You've got four stalls in the barn. It looks like it started in the stall closest to the back door."

"How could that be? There is nothing in that area but straw for the bedding, a couple of salt blocks and some tools like pitchforks, shovels and a wheelbarrow."

"Maybe a short in the wiring," the Chief suggested.

"As you can see this was a fairly new barn. There are no wires or electrical outlets or switches in that area. All the electrical outlets and switches are in the center or front of the barn or along the other wall. There are no wires running through the stalls, and all the wires running through the barn are in conduits so the horses, mice or any other critter can't accidentally eat through them."

"Hey, Chief," one of the fireman called out.

The Chief turned and looked at the fireman who called him and asked, "Yeah?"

"Looks like this fire was set. There's a gas can in here," the fireman said. "Looks like it might have been tossed through the window in the back door."

The Chief turned around, looked at Mark and said, "You got someone pissed off at you for something?"

Mark didn't answer him. He just looked at what was left of his barn. Setting a barn on fire when there were animals inside was the act of someone who was deranged. At the moment, Mark could think of one person who might be angry enough with him to do such a thing.

"Call the Sheriff," Mark said as he looked at the Chief.

"Oh, you can be sure the Sheriff will want to talk to you."

"No. I mean call him now, right now."

The Chief looked at Mark for a second, then turned and walked over to the fire truck. He had just pulled open the door and was reaching for the mike to his two-way radio when the Sheriff's car pulled up.

Mark saw the Sheriff drive up and started walking toward him. By now Mark was no longer in shock over the loss of his barn and the near loss of his horses. Instead he was mad as hell.

"What the hell are you going to do about this?" Mark blurted out angrily at the Sheriff.

"Take it easy. We'll get to the bottom of it," the Sheriff said in an effort to cool Mark's angry temper.

"That son of a bitch burned my barn down and damn near killed my horses."

"Settle down, Mr. Howard. We'll find out who did it."

"You know damn well who did it."

"No. I don't, but I can assure you that I will find out," the Sheriff said calmly, but with a tone of firmness in his voice.

"You better," Mark said.

"Are your horses okay?"

"They are for now."

"Okay. I want you to go back to the house and wait for me there. I need to talk to the Chief, then I'll want to have a talk with you," Sheriff Butler said.

Mark didn't want to leave, but there was nothing more he could do. Reluctantly, he turned and started back toward the house with Casey at his side.

Mark glanced back toward what was left of the barn before he got to the door of his house. He could see Sheriff Butler standing next to one of the fire trucks. He was talking with the Fire Chief. It was clear that the Fire Chief had a lot to say.

Mark opened the door and went into the ranch house. He began to think more clearly. He had jumped on the Sheriff pretty hard. The Sheriff had no idea what was going on and had nothing to go on. Sheriff Butler was a good man and he would do what was right.

Mark went into the kitchen and started a pot of coffee, then sat down to wait for the Sheriff. It wasn't long before the Sheriff knocked on the door.

"Come on in, the door's open," Mark said as he stood up.

Mark directed the Sheriff to the kitchen table as he poured the Sheriff and himself a cup of coffee. After setting the cups on the table, he sat down.

"Thanks," the Sheriff said as he wrapped his fingers around the cup.

"I'm sorry about blowing up at you out there," Mark said.

"It's okay. I understand," the Sheriff said.

"Well, what do you think?" Mark asked impatiently.

"I've got some questions for you."

"Go ahead."

"Do you normally keep gasoline in the barn?" the Sheriff asked.

"No. I don't keep any flammable liquids in the barn except for a bottle of Liniment I occasionally use on the horses for sore muscles. That bottle is, or I should say, was in a closed metal cabinet next to the front door."

"We both know who you think might have done this, but what I want to know is if there is anyone else that has threatened you lately, or is mad at you for some reason?"

Mark wondered what the Sheriff might be getting at, but he knew it was his job to look at all possibilities.

"No. Ah, wait a minute. No, I doubt she would do such a thing," Mark said shaking his head.

"Who is "she"?" the Sheriff asked.

"My ex-girl friend, Barbara Cooper."

"Barbara Cooper? Frank Cooper's daughter?" he asked with a tone of surprise in his voice.

"Yeah. We just broke up and she wasn't very happy about it."

"Do you think she might have been unhappy enough to burn your barn down?"

"I wouldn't think so," Mark replied, but he couldn't help but think about her hot temper.

"You look as if you're not sure."

"Well, I guess I'm not."

"What do you mean?"

"First of all, you have to know I've never seen her do anything violent or destructive before."

"But?"

"She does have a nasty temper."

"You mind explaining that?" the Sheriff asked.

"She called me earlier tonight. It was about dinnertime, say six or six-thirty. Anyway, when she finally seemed to get the message that it was over between us, she made a comment before she hung up," Mark said, not really wanting to tell the Sheriff what she had said.

"What did she say?"

"She said something to the effect that I would wish I hadn't done that to her. That I would wish I hadn't broken off our relationship," he explained.

"She was upset with you for breaking off your relationship?"

"Yes. She was pretty mad."

"Mad enough to burn your barn down?"

"God, I would hope not."

"In other words, you're not sure if she would burn your barn down or not if she felt it would get even with you for dropping her. Are you?"

Mark looked at Sheriff Butler as he thought about Barbara and the way she reacted to things that made her angry. The fact she didn't like his horses entered into his thoughts. He could not help but think the Sheriff might be right.

"I guess not," Mark answered.

"Well, the State Fire Marshall will be out here tomorrow morning to investigate the fire. We will have to wait and see what he comes up with. He may be able to help us find out who did it. I don't want you doing anything about this. I'll handle it. Do you understand?"

It was clear the Sheriff's comment was more than a suggestion, it was a warning. The Sheriff was right. He needed time to find out who had set the fire.

"Yes, I understand."

"Good. Now get a good night's sleep and go about your business tomorrow."

"I have to take care of my horses."

"Do you have a place you can keep them for a little while?"

"Yes, I think so. I'll put them in Miss Winters' barn for tonight. Her barn is empty and I don't think she would mind."

"Good. I'll get back to see you after the Fire Marshall gets his report to me."

Mark followed the Sheriff outside. As soon as the Sheriff had left, he went out to the pasture to round up his two horses. They were still a little skittish and he found them difficult to catch. Once he had them, he walked them over to Lora's barn where he bedded them down for the night.

By the time he returned home, it was late and the fire trucks were gone. He took a quick shower and went right to bed. As he laid in bed, he thought about Barbara. There was no question she had a nasty temper and didn't take rejection well, but could she burn his barn down? He thought about that for some time.

Mark knew Barbara didn't like his ranch and didn't care for his horses and his dog. He wondered if she thought if Mark didn't have the horses he might come back to her and be willing to move to Lodo. Even if she didn't like his horses and dog, he doubted she would try to kill them.

Mark was more inclined to think in terms of Jeff Bowman as the one who burned his barn down. He felt Bowman could do something like that as a way to send a message to Mark to stay away from Lora.

It proved hard for him to get to sleep. His mind was going full blast with reasons why someone would set his barn on fire. It was very late before sleep did finally come.

CHAPTER ELEVEN

It had been a short night for Mark and he had a lot to do before he was to go into town to pick up Lora. After feeding Casey and having his own breakfast, he slipped on his jacket and hat then went outside.

As he started to walk out toward the barn, he heard a car turn in the drive. Mark stopped and turned around to see who it was. The car was a large silver gray Lincoln Town Car. He immediately knew who was in the car. It was Barbara Cooper.

Mark let out a long sigh of disappointment at the thought of her coming here. He had hoped he would not have to deal with her today, or any other day for that matter. He had enough to do without having to put up with her and her temper.

The thought crossed his mind that Barbara might have come by to survey her handy work, but he quickly pushed that thought aside. He knew it wasn't fair for him to make accusations without some kind of proof. Besides, he was pretty sure she was not the type to dirty her pretty little hands by setting fire to his barn. She was more the type to get someone else to do it for her. Besides, he had no proof she was involved in any way with the burning of his barn.

"What are you doing here?" he asked rather bluntly as he walked toward the car.

Before she could answer him, another vehicle drove in the drive. Mark looked up and saw it was a bright red Chevy Tahoe with emergency lights on the roof. There was no doubt it was the State Fire Marshall and he was there to investigate the fire.

"Excuse me," Mark said as he glanced at Barbara.

Mark turned away from the Lincoln and walked toward the State Fire Marshall's vehicle without waiting for Barbara to acknowledge his comment. Mark wanted to talk to the Fire Marshall before he started his investigation.

As he walked toward the Fire Marshall's vehicle, it suddenly occurred to him that Barbara hadn't looked at all surprised to see the Fire Marshall there. It caused him to glance back over his shoulder at her. Barbara was just sitting in her Town Car watching

Mark as he approached the Fire Marshall's Vehicle.

"Good morning a tall man in his mid-fifties said as he got out of the Chevy Tahoe.

"Good morning. I take it you're here about the fire last night?"

"That's right. I'm Bill Salmon. I'm the State Fire Marshall."

"I'm Mark Howard. I own what's left of the barn."

"Well, I investigate all suspicious fires and this was reported to me as a suspicious fire."

"There's nothing suspicious about this fire. Someone set it on purpose."

"Oh, what makes you say that?" Salmon asked as he looked at Mark.

"One of the fireman found a gas can in the ruins of the barn. I have never kept gasoline in the barn."

"Oh, I see. And how do you think the gas can got there?"

"One of the firemen told the Chief it might have been tossed through the window in the back door. But I'm sure you would like to make that determination for yourself."

"Yes, I would," he replied with a smile.

"The barn's right around there," Mark said as he pointed toward what was left of it.

"Thank you."

"I'll be around for a little while, then I have to go get my horses, but I will be back shortly."

"That will be fine, Mr. Howard," he said, then walked around to the back of his Tahoe and got out a toolbox.

Mark turned and walked back over to Barbara's car. As he did, he noticed Barbara was watching the Fire Marshall as he walked off toward the remains of the barn.

"That's the State Fire Marshall," Mark said without taking his eyes off Barbara.

"Well, I came by to find out what it was that I did to cause you to want to end our relationship," she said in a calm voice.

There was no indication in her voice or in the expression on her face that she was even a slight bit interested in why the Fire Marshall was there. It was almost as if she already knew. Mark also knew from dating her that anything that didn't affect her personally, she paid little or no attention to, and had no interest in it.

"Listen, Barbara, I think you need to face the fact we don't have anything in common. You don't care for my horses, you don't like my dog and you don't like it up here. "I don't care to live in Denver and I don't think very much of several of your closest friends. Hell, we don't even like each other all that much. I think it's best we just end our relationship," Mark said.

"I see no reason to carry on. You should be out there finding yourself someone who likes the night life, the big city and likes the same things you like and will make you happy."

Barbara just sat in her car and looked at him while he spoke. The expression on her face gave no indication that what he was saying to her was even registering in her head.

"So, that's it?" she asked as if he had said nothing.

"Yes. That's it," he replied softly.

She turned her head and looked out the windshield for a moment. Without any warning, she reached over, put the car in reverse and slammed down on the gas pedal.

The tires spun and kicked up loose gravel as the car backed away from the house. Mark jumped back to avoid being hit by flying gravel. She stopped just short of hitting the Fire Marshall's Tahoe.

Barbara glared at Mark as she put the car in drive and hit the gas pedal again. The car once again kicked up loose gravel as the car sped down the drive to the road.

Mark stood there and watched as Barbara let her temper show. He was unimpressed by her childish behavior. In fact, the only good thing about the whole mess was that she was gone, and hopefully for good.

As soon as she was out of sight, Mark reached down and patted Casey on the head. He then turned around and started around toward the barn. Casey walked along side him.

As Mark walked past the barn, he could see Salmon kneeling down and digging around in the rubble of the barn. Mark stopped when Salmon stood up. He was examining something he had found. He was holding something small in his fingers as he turned it around and around while looking at it.

"Find something?" Mark called out to him.

Salmon turned and looked over at Mark, then looked back at what he was holding before he replied.

"Maybe," he said thoughtfully.

Mark walked over near the barn.

"What do you have?" Mark asked.

"I'm not sure, but it looks like some kind of curved metal clip. You got any idea what this is?" Salmon asked as he handed the small piece of blacken metal to Mark.

Mark examined it carefully. It looked familiar.

"I've seen something like this before," Mark said as he continued to examine it.

"Where?"

"I'm not sure," Mark said as he tried to remember.

"Well, it's evidence to me, so I'll keep it. If you remember where you've seen it and what it is, please let me know," Salmon said as he reached out his hand.

"I will," Mark said as he gave it back.

Salmon put the metal clip in an envelope, then returned to his work of digging around in the remains of the barn. Mark continued his walk across the pasture to Lora's barn.

Once Mark got to the barn, he took his horses out of the stalls and tied them to the fence outside. He went into the storage room in the barn to look for a shovel to clean the stalls his horses had used. Since he had not really had permission to use Lora's barn, he thought the least he could do was to clean up after his horses and put the barn back in order.

While in the storage room, he found a lot of old tools that hadn't been used in years. Some of them were a little rusty, but still serviceable. He knew that Wilbur Winters had had horses at one time, but not since he had know him. The barn hadn't been used in years for anything other than storage, although it was in pretty good shape.

As Mark reached for a shovel, another tool that hadn't been used for a long time caught his attention. It was hanging on the wall near the shovel. It was an old fashion lamplighter. It was used to light the oil lamps that hung from the ceiling or were high up on the wall where they would be hard to reach.

It had a wooden handle about two feet long. Attached to the end of the handle was a curved metal clip designed to hold a wooden matchstick.

Mark took the lamplighter off the wall and examined it. The metal end of it was rusty and badly worn. Although it was different from the one Salmon had found in the ruins of his barn, it quickly became clear that Salmon had found a lamplighter, at least the metal part of one. It was probably a little more modern than the one Mark found in Lora's barn, but a lamplighter just the same. Mark never had a lamplighter in his barn or his house.

Mark took the lamplighter and started back across the field toward his own barn. He was sure Salmon would want to see it. When he got there, he found Salmon smelling a piece of charred wood. Salmon looked up when he heard Mark coming toward him.

"Gasoline was used to accelerate the fire, maybe to start it," he said as Mark came up to him. "Most likely from the can found last night. From the looks of the can and the window, it was also used to break the rear window. I found pieces of broken glass from the window on the inside of the barn. If the window had been broken by the fire there would be pieces of glass outside the barn as well as inside. I didn't find any outside."

"What are you saying?"

"Based on what I have seen so far, this is the way I see it. Someone used the weight of a full can of gasoline to break the rear window. They then opened the can and tossed it inside the barn. They then tossed a match in through the window to light the fire. That is why the fire burned so quickly."

"That sounds good. I think you might be right up to where they tossed a match in to light the fire," Mark said as he held up the lamplighter.

"What do you have there?" Salmon asked.

"I believe this is what was used to start the fire. Well not this one, but one just like it," Mark said.

"What is that?"

"It's a lamplighter. They were used to light oil lamps that were high and hard to reach. It holds a match in the end. One like this could have been used to start the fire, then tossed in the barn. I would think that tossing just a match through a window would not assure the match would make it to the floor before going out. A tool like this would give someone enough reach to start the fire without the danger of the gasoline blowing up in their face or the match going out before it could start the gasoline. I think you will find the clip you found in the barn is very much like this one," Mark said as he handed the lamplighter to Salmon to inspect.

Salmon looked over the lamplighter and then compared it to the clip he found in the ruins. He looked up at Mark and smiled.

"Where did you get this?"

"I found it in my neighbor's barn. That one is very old, but I would be willing to bet the clip you found is a more modern version of one of these."

"Can I have it?" Salmon asked.

"I'm sorry, but it's not mine to give."

"I'll return it to you in a few days. I want to find out where such a thing can be purchased."

"I would start with stores selling fireplace equipment," Mark suggested.

"Good idea. I'll get this back to you when I'm finished."

"Okay. Do you need me any more for awhile?"

"No, I don't think so. One thing. Did you have one of these lamplighters?"

"No. I've never had one," Mark replied.

"What about a gas can? Do you own one of those?"

"Yes, I do. It's in my workshop."

"Are you sure?"

"Yes. I'll show you."

Mark started toward his workshop and Salmon followed along behind. Mark unlocked the door to the shop and opened it. He then stood back as he pointed to an old round red can sitting on a shelf just inside the shed door. Salmon leaned inside the shed and looked at the can.

"It's still here," he said as he reached in and picked it up. "It's almost full," Salmon said as he looked at Mark.

"Yes. I filled it just the other day. I use it for the lawn mower."

"I see," Salmon said as he set the can back on the shelf.

"Is there anything else I can do for you?"

"No, not for the moment," Salmon replied. "I'll be finished here in a little while. I'll be in touch, though."

"I'm sure," Mark replied.

Mark turned around and headed back to the barn on Lora's property. After cleaning out the barn, he untied his horses and led them back to his ranch where he turned them out in the pasture.

When Mark returned to his ranch, he noticed the Fire Marshall was still digging through the ruins of the barn. Mark figured it would take him the better part of the day to go through all of it. He thought about stopping to talk to Salmon, but changed his mind. He felt Salmon knew what he was doing and didn't need someone interrupting him. Besides, Salmon would have to return to his office or lab to process any evidence he found before he could prove anything.

A quick look at his watch told Mark that it was getting on toward lunchtime. He just had time enough to get cleaned up and get to the hospital before noon.

As he drove into town, Mark's mind was going back and forth between Jeff and Barbara. He felt he didn't know Jeff well enough to know if he would be the type who would burn a barn down just to make a point. But if he was, what was the point he was trying to make? Was he trying to get Mark to stay away from Lora? That seemed very believable. After all he had threatened Mark once before and told him that he would be the one running Mark off Lora's property.

He had to ask himself the same questions about Barbara. Was she capable of burning down his barn just because she was upset with him? Mark had seen her temper a good many times. She was about as spoiled a woman as Mark had ever met. It had always been easy for her to get anything she wanted. Putting those two things together, it was believable.

Mark hated to admit it, but there were two people who he felt were suspects in the burning of his barn. Even though their motives were different, either one of them might have done it.

Mark was getting close to the hospital. He didn't want his thoughts about who had burned his barn to cloud Lora and his afternoon. He would take her to lunch and then to the grocery store before he took her to her ranch. Once she was settled in and comfortable, he would tell her about the barn and ask her if he could keep his horses at her ranch for a little while.

He felt it was the best approach. She had enough on her mind without him springing it all on her right away. Besides, he wanted her to move closer to him where he could check in on her every day until she was able to take care of herself. If he told her about all his problems, she might decide to stay in town instead.

Mark pulled into the parking lot of the hospital and began to look for a parking space. As he turned down a row of cars, he saw a parking space near the end of the row. He drove down to it and pulled into the space. As he was getting out of his truck, he saw a black BMW sedan a couple of spaces from the end. His first thought was that it might be Jeff Bowman's car.

He took a deep breath and started walking toward the front of the hospital. Mark kept a close watch for Bowman. He didn't want to be surprised by him.

As Mark walked into the lobby, he looked around half expecting to see Jeff. He didn't see anyone in the lobby he recognized. It was a relief for Mark not to see Jeff in the lobby, but it was hard for Mark to get the thought that he was somewhere in the hospital.

Mark went over to the elevator and pushed the button. As he waited for the elevator, he looked around the lobby some more. The lobby had very few people in it. While he was looking, he noticed another black BMW go by outside. It was not the same one he had seen in the parking lot. With the glare and the tined windows on the car, he could not make out who was in it.

The bell of the elevator rang, disturbing his thoughts. He turned around and waited for the doors to open. He stepped in and pressed the button for the third floor. Just as the doors were closing he caught a glimpse of Jeff coming in the front door of the hospital. Damn, he thought. The last thing he wanted was any trouble in front of Lora, even though he would not mind punching Jeff's lights out.

As much as the thought of punching Jeff in the nose appealed to him, he would much rather have a court of law do it for him. If Jeff was the one that burned down his barn and the Fire Marshall could prove it, it would be much more satisfying to see Jeff lose his license to practice law and go to jail.

As the elevator arrived on the third floor and the door started to open, Mark thought it might be a good idea if he told Lora that Jeff was in the building. He felt she should know. If she still didn't want to see him, they could go out by another exit.

Mark stepped off the elevator and turned down the hall toward Lora's room. As he passed the nurse's station, one of the nurses called to him.

"Excuse me, but are you Mark Howard?" the nurse asked.

Mark turned around and walked back to the nurse's station before he responded.

"Yes."

"Miss Winters asked me to tell you that she is downstairs at the Discharge Desk."

"The Discharge Desk?"

"Yes. It is located off the lobby. She is signing her insurance forms for her release. She asked us to tell you that she would meet you there."

"Thank you," Mark said, then turned around and went back to the elevator.

As he approached the elevator, he thought about Jeff. There was a very good chance he could run into him if he took the elevator back to the lobby. Mark quickly decided he would take the chance and take the elevator. He would simply get on the next elevator that he could use to take down. If he ran into Jeff, he would let him get off while he got on. If he was lucky, by the time Jeff figured out Mark had gotten on the elevator right behind him and that Lora was probably already downstairs, it would be too late.

Just then the bell of the elevator rang. Mark moved up next to the doors and waited for them to open. When the doors opened he turned his back toward the doors while Jeff stepped off the elevator. Then Mark quickly turned and moved past Jeff. He had hoped that by the time Jeff realized it was Mark the elevator doors would be closing.

Mark stepped into the elevator and quickly pressed the button to close the doors and to send the elevator to the lobby. Just before the doors closed, Mark saw Jeff had stopped and was turning around. The last thing Mark saw was Jeff starting to reach for the doors, but it was too late. It had worked.

When the elevator stopped at the lobby and the doors opened, Mark hurried out of the elevator and across the lobby to the Discharge Desk. He found Lora sitting in front of a desk in a wheelchair while the person behind the desk typed on a computer.

Lora glanced over her shoulder and saw Mark coming toward her. She smiled at him as he approached the office, but her smile faded away rather quickly when she saw the look on his face. She had a feeling there was something wrong.

"Hi," she said to him as he entered the office.

"Hi. Are you about finished here?"

"I'll be just a moment," the lady behind the computer said with a smile.

Mark sat down on a chair next to Lora, then glanced over his shoulder toward the elevators. He then turned back around and looked at Lora. He wasn't real sure what he should say, but he thought it was best to tell her.

"I think you should know Jeff is here."

"Where?" Lora asked, the look on her face telling Mark that she really didn't want to deal with him.

"I passed him at the elevator on the third floor. He was getting off and I was getting on to come here. My guess is he will be down here any minute."

"I don't want to see him," she said her eyes pleading with Mark to find a way so she didn't have to deal with him.

Mark reached out and put his hand over her hand and smiled. He hoped it would help her to know he understood how she felt. The last thing he wanted to do was to have a confrontation with Jeff in front of her.

It took another few minutes for Lora to get all the paperwork done so she could leave. When she was ready, Mark stood up. As he did, he could see Jeff standing half way across the lobby watching them. From the look in his eyes, Mark was sure he was angry. It was obvious he didn't like the fact Mark was with Lora. Mark moved around behind Lora's wheelchair but didn't move her.

"Excuse me," Mark said to the lady behind the desk. "Would you mind calling for a security guard."

"Is there a problem?" the woman asked.

"Not yet, and I would like to avoid one."

The lady behind the desk had a puzzled look on her face, but picked up the phone. Lora turned her head and looked up at Mark. She wasn't sure it was a good idea, but if Mark thought it was then she would go along with it.

It wasn't long before the guard showed up in the office.

"Is there a problem, sir?" he asked.

"No, not really. I would prefer to prevent one."

"You mind explaining that?"

"Miss Winters had given instructions that her ex-boyfriend was not to be allowed to visit her. He happens to be standing in the lobby right now," Mark said.

The guard looked out into the lobby. He saw Jeff suddenly look away.

"Is that your ex-boyfriend?" he asked Lora

"Yes," Lora replied.

"Do you wish not to see him?"

"Yes."

"Do you have a restraining order to keep him away from you?"

"No, sir," she replied looking up at the guard.

"I can only keep him away from you while you are on the hospital grounds, but I cannot do anything else. Might I suggest you obtain a restraining order as soon as possible? If you had a restraining order, I could have him arrested if he bothers you," the security guard explained.

"Thank you," Lora said meekly.

"I can escort you to your car if you like."

"Thank you, I would like that."

"Come with me," he said and then turned to leave the office.

Mark started pushing her out of the office behind the guard. Jeff started to come toward them. The guard signaled for Mark to stop, then stepped toward Jeff putting himself between Jeff and Lora. He put his hand up to stop Jeff.

"Sir, I would suggest you come no closer to Miss Winters, or I will have you arrested," the guard said quietly but firmly.

"You can not prevent me from talking to my girlfriend," Jeff insisted.

"I can if she does not want to talk to you."

"Do you know who I am?" Jeff said sharply to the guard with a threatening tone in his voice.

"No, sir, and I don't care who you are. If you insist on disrupting her departure from this hospital, I will have you arrested," the guard said without even a hint of backing down.

"I'm an attorney," Jeff said sharply.

With that the guard raised his hand and motioned to another guard to join him. He continued to stand between Lora and Jeff while he waited for the other guard to come over and see what was going on.

"Bill, escort this man over to the security office and keep him there until I return. I will be back in a couple of minutes to fill out a complaint to send to the police department. I want it on file that this man was harassing Miss Winters while she was under the care of this hospital."

"Yes, sir," Bill replied.

"You can't do that," Jeff said angrily.

"If you're any kind of an attorney at all, you know darn well I can," he said, then motioned for the guard to take him to the security office.

"Come with me, sir," Bill said.

When Jeff made no move to go with the guard, Bill said, "We can do this the easy way or the hard way. Either way is fine with me."

Jeff looked at Bill's face. It was clear Bill was prepared to put him in cuffs if he didn't comply with the order. Jeff reluctantly gave in.

While Jeff was being led off to the security office, the guard turned and looked at Lora in the wheelchair.

"If you don't need my assistance any more, I'll return to my office."

"Thank you. Thank you very much," Lora said looking up at him.

"Thanks," Mark said.

"You're welcome. Have a nice day," he said then turned and started off toward his office.

"I hope Jeff doesn't get into too much trouble," Lora said.

"Why? He brought it on himself," Mark said as he began pushing her wheelchair toward the front door.

"I know, but it could have an effect on his career."

"Whatever effect it has on his career, he brought on himself. In case you hadn't noticed, he has a nasty temper."

Lora didn't say anything more. This past week had been very hard on her. Regardless of what Mark said, she had loved Jeff. It was not easy for her to simply dismiss him from her mind. It was even harder for her to forget what he had done to her by having an affair with his secretary.

CHAPTER TWELVE

When Mark got her to his pickup, he opened the door. He leaned down, put his arms around her and picked her up out of the wheelchair.

"You don't have to do this. I can stand up," Lora said.

"I know," Mark replied as he carefully set her down on the seat.

Mark reached around her and hooked her seatbelt for her. After closing the truck door, he put her wheelchair in the back of the pickup. He went around, got in and backed out of the parking space.

As he drove out of the parking lot onto the street, he glanced over at her. She was looking straight ahead. He was sure she was thinking about what had just happened.

Mark began to think about what he had said and was sure it had upset her a little. He knew the whole thing had to be difficult for her. She hadn't told him about what Jeff had done. What little information he had was all secondhand.

He decided he might have spoken out of turn. She would tell him what she wanted him to know. He had no right to pry into her personal affairs.

"Where would you like to go for lunch?" Mark asked in the hope of getting her to talk to him.

"I guess I'm not very hungry. Would it be all right if you took me home?" she said softly, her voice giving him some clue as to how she was feeling at the moment.

"Sure," he said, a little disappointed and a little upset with himself for being so frank about Jeff.

Mark was not happy about her decision to simply go home, but she had a lot on her mind. He had not made things easy for her, either. Maybe he had expected too much.

Mark drove out onto the Interstate and headed up to the mountains. It was a quiet ride, as Lora seemed to be off in another world. She didn't have much to say and it appeared to Mark that she didn't want to talk.

When he drove into the drive at her ranch, he pulled up in front of the house and stopped. He looked at her for a second before he got out of the truck. Mark took her wheelchair out of the back and placed it next to the truck. He opened the door and leaned in to pick her up.

"I can do it," she insisted.

Mark looked at her for a minute before he stepped back. He braced the door for her and watched as she swung her legs out over the side. She then stood up on her one good foot and turned herself around. Mark reached out and pulled the wheelchair closer to her and held it while she sat down.

He wheeled her to the front door and took the key he had gotten from the under the urn and unlocked the door. He pushed the door open, handed her the key, then pushed her wheelchair into the house.

Lora looked around the living room as she entered the house. It had been a long time since she had been here. She never really understood why she hadn't moved up here. It would have saved her money and she always liked it here.

She looked around and soaked in all that was familiar about the place. She remembered how much she liked coming up here as a child and playing in the woods out beyond the pasture.

"Where would you like to be?" Mark asked.

"Right here will be fine," she said with a smile, but she didn't look all that sincere.

"Are you sure?"

"Yes."

"What would you like? I'd be more than happy to fix you something to eat, but I'll have to go home to fix it. We didn't stop to get groceries. I forgot all about it until just now," he said apologetically.

"That's okay, I'm fine. What I would really like is to be left alone for a while," she said as she looked at him.

The last thing she wanted to do was to hurt his feelings, but she needed time to be alone with her thoughts. She hoped Mark would understand.

"Oh, ah, I guess I'll go take care of my horses," he said, not knowing what else he could say at the moment.

"Thank you for everything."

"Sure. No problem. I'll just leave my phone number here on the table in case you need me."

"Okay," she said, but didn't look at him.

Mark looked at her for a second, then turned and left the house. As he walked to the truck, he couldn't help but think of her all alone and without any food in the house. He decided he would fix her something later and take it to her.

The other thing bothering Mark was the fact Jeff knew where she was living. If he decided to come up here and see her, there was no way she could stop him. Mark was convinced that if Jeff decided to see her, he would do anything it took including breaking into her house.

Mark got into his truck and started it up. He took one last look at the house before he put the truck in gear and drove out the driveway. There was nothing else he could do for now. If she wanted to be alone, that was her business.

Lora sat in her wheelchair and watched Mark through the living room window as he walked out to his truck. She was having a hard time understanding her feelings of anger. She was sending him away, but why? He had done nothing but try to help her from the very first moment they met. He had asked nothing of her except to be friends. If she were truly honest with herself, she would realize he had not even asked for that.

She was also feeling a bit guilty. Lora owed him so much, but maybe that was the problem. She didn't like owing anyone anything. The fact that her life was such a mess didn't help any.

Part of her feeling of guilt might be because she had never told Mark what had happened the night of the accident. He seemed to know something about it, but she had not told him her side of the story or any of the details.

Lora looked around the living room and thought how nice a job Mark had done in cleaning her house and making it a welcome place for her to recuperate. She wheeled herself over to the sofa by pulling herself along with her one good foot. Once she was at the sofa, she stood up, turned around and sat down.

After lying down, she took the afghan off the back of the sofa and spread it over herself. She laid there looking up at the ceiling.

Her mind began to relive what had happened over the past few days. Tears came to her eyes as she thought about Jeff and how he had treated her. She thought about Jeff at the hospital and how he refused to let go. She couldn't comprehend how Jeff couldn't understand it was over between them and that she never wanted to see him again.

Lora had not had the happiest of lives. In her short life she had had two men that she loved and both of them had been unfaithful to her. They had cheated on her.

Then there was her father whom she had not seen since she was ten years old. She had not realized it, but he was as much a part of the way she was feeling toward men as the other two. She had gotten up one morning to find he had walked out on her and her mother without so much as saying goodbye.

Her thoughts turned to Mark. He had been kind, helpful, and appeared to be a real gentleman. But what was he really like? Was he like the others?

Lora had no real reason to believe Mark was any different, but then why would she think he would be? She had not had the experience of having a good loyal man. In short, she had no positive experiences with men, at least not on a long term bases.

Lora decided that she would keep Mark at arms length. She would not give him the chance to break her heart like the others.

It occurred to her that he might not want to come back and see her again, anyway. She had not treated him very well. If he looked closely at their relationship up to now, he would see she had done nothing to make him want to get to know her. And if he looked really close, he might even think she had been using him. Something in the back of her mind told her that Mark would not like it.

Lora closed her eyes and tried to go to sleep, but sleep would not come. She was having a hard time getting Mark off her mind. As much as she didn't like the idea, she was beginning to realize she might actually like him. Although Lora felt Mark might like her, she was sure he had no idea how she really felt about him. If it were up to her, she would not let him know. She also realized that until she got Jeff off her mind and out of her life, there was no sense even thinking about Mark.

What Jeff had done to her was too close, too real, and too hurtful for her to forget it so quickly. It would be a long time before she would be able to get the sight of Jeff and his secretary out of her head.

The thought of Jeff caused Lora to open her eyes, turn her head and look at the front door. She could see the door was unlocked. She wondered if Jeff knew about her ranch in the foothills. She had not told him about inheriting it from her grandfather. She had planned to make it a wedding gift.

It suddenly occurred to her it would not be very hard for Jeff to find out about the ranch. After all, he often had lunch with attorneys from the law firm that handled her grandfather's will. If one of them knew about the ranch and knew he was dating her, he might have let it out that Lora had a ranch in the foothills.

There was also the possibility he knew from the newspapers. She would have been mentioned as the next of kin. In fact, she was the only kin to the old man. She knew Jeff read the newspaper very closely every day. He was always looking for ways to bring new clients to the law firm. He had often told her that the more business he could produce for the firm, the better his chances of getting a partnership in the firm.

If Jeff did know about the ranch, she thought he might come to the ranch when he couldn't find her at her town house. The last thing she wanted was to have him confront her when she was all alone. She didn't think she could deal with him right now.

It also occurred to her that if Jeff knew that Mark lived down the road a little ways, he might even get more upset with her. She had seen their confrontation at the hospital. She had no idea how violent Jeff could get, but if what happened in the hospital lobby was any indication she didn't want any part of him.

Lora sat up, swung herself around and stood up in front of her wheelchair. She turned around and sat down in it. She then pulled herself to the door. She locked the door by locking the doorknob and turning the dead bolt to make sure the door was secure.

As she turned around to go back to the sofa, she wondered if the back door was locked. She wheeled herself out through the kitchen to the back door. She locked and secured that door as well.

Feeling much more secure about being locked in the house, she began to wheel herself back to the living room. When she got to the living room, she began to realize that she had locked herself in. Although, she was feeling safer, she was also felling like a prisoner in her own home.

She let the feeling pass, then returned to the sofa. At least being locked in her own house she would be able to get some rest. She laid down and covered herself again with the afghan. It wasn't long and she was asleep.

When Mark drove into the drive of his ranch, he saw the Fire Marshall standing near his truck. He wondered if he had finished with his work. He wasn't the least bit worried about what he might find. After all, he had not set his own barn on fire.

Casey was sitting at the front door. The Fire Marshall was loading his things into his truck as Mark pulled up in front of the house. Mark got out and walked over to him.

"Are you finished checking over the barn?" Mark asked.

"Yes, at least for now."

"Did you find anything else you can't identify?"

"No, but I know how the fire started."

"How?"

"Pretty much the way we talked about. It was set on purpose."

"I already knew that. Did you find anything that might help you catch the person responsible for the fire?"

"Maybe, but I'd rather not say at the moment. I do have a few questions for you. Would you mind if we cover them now?"

"No, not at all. Have you had lunch?"

"No, not yet."

"Why don't you come over to the house and we'll grab a bite to eat and you can ask me anything you want. I haven't had lunch yet, either."

"Okay," Salmon agreed.

Salmon followed Mark into the house. Mark directed him to have a seat at the kitchen table.

"Sandwiches okay?"

"Sure."

"Go ahead and ask your questions while I fix a couple of sandwiches. What would you like to drink?"

"Milk would be nice, if you have it, otherwise water will do."

"I've got milk. Go ahead and ask your questions."

"Okay. Is the barn insured?"

"Yes, for the replacement cost," Mark replied as he spread dressing on the bread.

"Are you required to replace the barn?"

"No, I don't think so. But if I don't replace it, where am I going to keep my horses?"

"I see your point. Do you have any enemies, Mr. Howard?"

"Well, I wouldn't say I have enemies, no."

"Anyone one that might be upset or angry with you?"

"I can think of a couple of people that are not too happy with me at the moment, but I doubt they would be pissed off enough to burn down my barn and possibly kill my horses."

"Are you sure?"

"I guess no one is really sure of what someone might do under any given circumstances," Mark said as he set a plate with a ham and cheese sandwich down in front of Salmon.

"Some people will do strange things to get even with someone for something they believe they did," Salmon said as Mark sat down across the table from him."

"I guess you're right about that," Mark admitted.

"Would you mind telling me who might be upset with you?" Salmon asked then took a bite of the sandwich.

Mark let out a long sigh before he answered.

"As I told the Sheriff, there are two people that are upset with me at the moment. One of them I have no idea what he would do if he thought I was a threat to him in some way. The other I can't see her burning down my barn or attempting to kill my horses, even though I know she doesn't really care for them or this ranch."

"Who are these people?" Salmon asked.

"One of them is my ex-girlfriend. I told the Sheriff about her last night."

"Why don't you tell me about her?" Salmon asked.

"We broke up yesterday. She said she was going to make me sorry for ending our relationship. Her name is Barbara Cooper."

"Frank Cooper's daughter?" Salmon asked with surprise.

"The very same one. You know them?"

"I sure do."

"Well then, you know how spoiled she is," Mark said.

"Yes, I do. Who's the other one?"

"Jeff Bowman. He's an attorney."

"I don't know him. What's he like?"

"He's got a mean temper."

"How are you connected to him?"

"I wouldn't say I'm connected to him. It seems he is the ex-boyfriend of Lora Winters. She's the woman who drove her car off the road and into the canyon just down my drive."

"Oh, yes. I read about it in the paper. It didn't mention Bowman was her boyfriend."

"Ex-boyfriend. The way the sheriff explained it to me was she caught her boyfriend in the arms of another women. I get the impression from him, and with what he did at the hospital, that he has a nasty temper. He threatened to toss me off Miss Winters's ranch once she came to her senses and returned to him. By the way, Miss Winters owns the ranch just up the road. I met him there one afternoon when I went over to make sure the house was secured."

"Is that when he threatened you," Salmon asked.

"Yes."

"It seems to me that I have a couple of likely suspects," Salmon said as he took another bite of the sandwich.

"I know I'm one of them."

"What makes you think that?"

"I owned the barn, it was insured, the horses are insured, what more do I have to say?" Mark said as the looked across the table at Salmon.

"I see your point, but I'm not looking at you as my prime suspect. In fact, I don't have a prime suspect at the moment. I still have a lot of work to do. Let me ask you one more question."

"Fire away, excuse the pun," Mark said with a smile.

"If you build a new barn, are you going to build one that is, say, bigger?"

"No. I have no reason to build a bigger barn. As a matter of fact, I would build one just like the old one. As you may have noticed, the barn isn't really very old. It was built only two years ago. It was big enough for what I need even if I were to get a couple more horses, which are not in my current plans. What makes you ask?"

"Usually, if a person burns down their own building it is to get the money to build something bigger or better, or it is to collect the insurance money and not rebuild."

"If you read my policy, I don't get full value of the barn unless I rebuild it."

"I have already checked your policy on the barn. You are correct. It only pays for the replacement value, not the actual value, if you rebuild. The difference can be rather a large amount depending on the age and size of the building."

The talk between Mark and Salmon turned to the subject of Jeff Bowman and Barbara Cooper as they finished their lunch. Salmon seemed to be interested in Jeff Bowman more than in Barbara. Mark thought that might be because he seemed to know a little about the Cooper family, and apparently didn't know anything about Bowman.

Mark had a hard time seeing Barbara as the one who burned down his barn. It wasn't that he didn't feel she was capable of doing it. It was more she didn't seem to be the type to destroy something simply to prove a point. He felt that she was more the type to cause problems between him and any new woman that he might take an interest in, at least until she found someone else to direct her attention toward.

On the other hand, Bowman had the kind of temperament that made Mark think he was capable of doing anything he felt would be necessary to get the results he wanted. Mark was inclined to look at Jeff as the one who had burned his barn down and almost killed his horses.

"I'm glad I don't have your job," Mark said.

"I sometimes wish I didn't have it either," Salmon said with a grin.

"You'd have a hard time convincing me that you don't like what you do."

"I really do most of the time. It's very rewarding when I find out who set a fire and bring them to justice. It has its moments though."

"I'm sure it does, but what job doesn't." Mark replied.

"Good point. I guess I best be getting on my way. I have a lot of things to examine and tests to run before I will know what happened and who did it," Salmon said as he stood up. "Thanks for the lunch."

"You're welcome. I enjoyed talking with you," Mark said as he stood up. "Feel free to stop by any time."

Mark followed Salmon to the door and watched him as he walked to his Tahoe. Mark wondered what Salmon was going to find. He couldn't help but think about Barbara. He hoped it was not some of her work or the work of someone she hired. He would hate to find out he had been going with a woman capable of setting his barn on fire and almost killing his horses just because she was mad at him.

As soon as the Fire Marshall was gone, Mark returned to the kitchen. He cleaned up the kitchen and then went to his computer to put the finishing touches on his article for the week.

CHAPTER THIRTEEN

Time passed rather quickly for Mark as he sat at his computer and finished his article for the newspaper. He was ready to fax it off to the newspaper, but a quick look at his watch told him it was already after six o'clock. He remembered he had not gone to the store to get groceries for Lora. She would have nothing in the house to eat.

Mark shut down his computer for the night and went out to the kitchen. He wasn't sure what he should fix Lora for dinner. He had no idea how hungry she might be or what she liked. Mark decided the best thing was for him to fix her something easy and filling, and then take it over to her. If she didn't want to eat, he could leave it with her so she could have it later if she changed her mind.

He fixed Casey's dinner then fixed dinner for Lora and himself. If she didn't feel like eating or didn't want him around, he could come back home. He prepared a couple of hamburgers with all the trimmings then wrapped them up to keep them warm. He grabbed a bottle of Pepsi from the refrigerator to take along. It wasn't much but it was what he would have fixed for himself.

As soon as it was ready, he started toward Lora's ranch house with Casey at his side. As he walked, he remembered he had not asked her if he could bed his horses down in her barn until he could get a new barn built. He thought it might be as good a time as any to ask her.

As he came around the end of a row of trees near the side of the house, he could see a black BMW parked out in front. He knew Jeff was there. His first thought was to turn around and go back home, but he was not sure if Lora could handle Jeff alone.

As he moved around the end of the trees and started for the front of the house, he could hear someone. It was a man's voice and it seemed to be speaking rather harshly. Mark set the hamburgers and Pepsi down on a bench near the back corner of the house, told Casey to stay and walked around to the front.

"Lora, you're making too much of this. She doesn't mean anything to me," Jeff said, his voice pleading with her, yet there was an underlying anger in his words.

There was a pause before anything else was said.

"Lora, you're going to have to talk to me sooner or later. You might as well open the door so I can explain. I know you will understand."

Mark waited and watched for a minute to see if Lora was going to open the door. He wanted to know if Lora was going to let Jeff in or not.

"Damn that woman," Mark heard Jeff say under his breath.

"Go away," he heard Lora call out from inside the house. "Go away and leave me alone."

"Damn it, Lora, open the damn door," Jeff yelled.

That did it as far as Mark was concerned. He felt it was getting to the point where Jeff might decide to try and break into Lora's house. He was not about to let that happen.

"I don't think she wants to talk to you," Mark said as he stepped out from around the corner of the house.

Jeff swung around. He had a surprised look on his face at seeing Mark only a few paces behind him.

"You again," Jeff said angrily. "You just can't keep you damn nose out of other people's business, can you?"

"Not when they force me into it," Mark said calmly.

"What's that supposed to mean?"

"Let's deal with one thing at a time. Miss Winters has no interest in seeing you. I think she has made that very clear."

"She will see me whether you like it or not," Jeff insisted.

"I'd like to know just one thing. Have you always been this stupid or did you have to learn it over the years? Wake up. She doesn't want to see you any more. Now I would suggest you leave before this turns into a real problem for you."

"What, you planning on making me leave?" Jeff said with a hint of a chuckle in his voice.

"If you press it, yes," Mark replied.

"Well I don't think you can, cowboy," Jeff said as he stepped closer to Mark.

Mark didn't back up an inch. If Jeff was going to get physical, Mark was not about to back away. He had no proof, but Mark was sure it had been Jeff who had burned down his barn. He would like nothing more than to flatten Jeff's nose against his face, but he would not take the first shot.

"Before you try to beat me to a pulp, I'd like to know how it felt to burn my barn down and almost kill my horses."

"You think I did that?" Jeff said with a grin. "You'll have to prove it."

"That's what the Fire Marshall is working on."

"You accusing me of that? I'll sue your pants off if you try. Then I'll own both places."

"So that's it. You don't give a damn about Lora. All you want is her ranch. I'm sure she will be glad to hear that."

"You're not going to be around to tell her," Jeff said as he stepped up closer to Mark.

Although Mark's hands were at his sides, he was ready for whatever Jeff might try. Jeff turned slightly and looked over his shoulder toward the house, then without any warning he quickly turned back around and took a swing at Mark.

Mark ducked the swing and sent out a sharp jab that caught Jeff on the end of his nose, breaking his nose and sending blood all over. It also knocked Jeff on his butt. Mark did not take advantage of Jeff, he simply stepped back a step or two and waited to see what Jeff was going to try next.

Jeff turned over and got up on his hands and knees and then turned his head and looked up at Mark. There was hatred in his eyes. Mark could not see it, but Jeff grabbed a handful of dirt and tossed it at Mark's face. Mark tried to duck, but still got some of the dirt in his eyes.

Jeff jumped up and rushed at Mark. Still finding it hard to see, Mark dropped down as Jeff rushed at him. When he felt Jeff stumble against him, he raised up quickly sending Jeff in a cartwheel over him. Jeff landed on his back with a thud, knocking the wind out of him.

As Jeff was trying to get up, the front door of the house opened. Lora stood on one leg in the doorway leaning against the doorjamb.

"Stop it. Stop it, both of you," she yelled, her voice showing she was almost in tears.

Mark turned and looked at Lora. He could see the hurt look in her eyes. The last thing he wanted was for her to see him fighting, but Jeff had started it and he was only defending himself.

"Jeff, go away and leave me alone. If you come back here I'll have you arrested for harassing me and for tresspassing," she said sharply.

"But honey, I can explain," Jeff said like a whiny little child.

"No you can't. You will never be able to explain away what you did to me. I never want to see you again. Now go before I call the police," she insisted.

Jeff stood up straight and looked at her. He was angry with her, but he was angrier with himself. It was now over between them. He would not get her back and he would not get control of the ranch.

Mark stood there and watched as Jeff brushed off his suit as he walked to his car. He waited until Jeff started the car and drove away, then he turned around toward Lora.

"I don't think you will have any more trouble with him," Mark said as he brushed the dirt off the front of his shirt.

"I would appreciate it if you would go, too," Lora said sharply.

"But I came to bring you something to eat. Why are you sending me away? Jeff took a swing at me first," Mark asked, confused by her reaction. "I'm not supposed to defend myself?"

"Because you men are all the same," she said angrily.

"What? He must have done a real number on you. Well, if that's the way you feel, I certainly won't force myself on you," Mark said angrily as he turned and started to walk back the way he had come.

Lora stood there and watched him as he stormed off. She knew he was upset with her, but she couldn't deal with it now. He then stopped and looked back over his shoulder at her.

"I have something for you, then I promise I will go and leave you alone," Mark said, his voice showing he was not only angry, but he was hurt.

Mark stepped around the corner of the house and picked up the hamburgers and Pepsi he had left there. He took them over to her and handed them to her.

Lora looked at the hamburgers and the Pepsi, and then looked up at him.

"It's your dinner. I know you don't have anything in the house to eat," he said as he held it out to her.

She hesitated for a moment then reached out and took them.

"I won't bother you any more," Mark said flatly, then turned sharply and walked away without looking back.

Lora stood and watched him as he disappeared around the corner of the house. Once he was gone, she looked at the dinner he had fixed for her. With so much food, she was sure he had planned on eating with her.

Lora turned around and sat down in her wheelchair. She put her dinner in her lap, reached out, closed the door and locked it.

She looked down at the dinner, but she was not feeling very hungry. It seemed to her no matter what she did, it was not turning out very well. She wheeled herself to the kitchen and put her dinner in the refrigerator. Lora would eat it later, if she was feeling hungry.

Lora spent the rest of the evening lying on the sofa, most of the time with tears in her eyes. All she could think about was how messed up her life was, and how much of it was her own fault.

Mark walked back to his ranch house. He was angry at the way things had turned out. His mind was going a mile a minute. He made a decision as he walked back toward his house, a decision he would stick to no matter what. His decision was not to go over to Lora's ranch unless she invited him. If she had a problem or needed something, she would have to ask for his help. He was not going to offer to help her any more.

As he crossed the pasture to his house, he saw his horses. He had no barn to put them in for the night. Mark looked up at the sky. It was a clear night with lots of stars. He remembered that the weather was supposed to be nice for the next few days. The horses could stay outside for a few nights. A lot of the horses around here did when the weather was nice.

Mark went to his storage shed and found a couple of buckets. He put a little grain mixture in each of the buckets and took them over to the fence. He set them inside the fence for the horses. He then got some hay for each of them and put it over the fence.

He leaned against the wooden fence and watched as the horses slowly meandered over to the buckets and began eating. He really wasn't paying much attention to the horses. He was too busy thinking about Lora. Maybe it was time for him to forget about her and go about his business. If she wanted to talk to him or see him, she had his phone number. She could call.

Mark turned away from the fence, walked to the house and went inside. As he was walking through the kitchen, his phone began to ring. He stopped and looked at it, but was hesitant to answer it. He was not sure if he was ready to talk to Lora, but on the other hand he had told her if she needed anything she should call. The one thing Mark would not do was go back on his word.

Mark stepped over next to the counter and picked up the phone.

"Hello," he said without much enthusiasm.

"What the hell do you think you're doing?" an angry female voice came screaming over the phone.

Mark knew instantly it was Barbara. It took him a minute to figure out what it was she might be mad at him for this time. Then it hit him. The Fire Marshall must have questioned her.

"Nothing," he replied casually.

"What do you mean "nothing"? The Fire Marshall came to my house and parked that big red truck of his right in front of the house where everyone could see it. And then he had the gall to question me as if I was a common criminal," she yelled into the phone.

"You're anything but common."

"What's that supposed to mean."

"Nothing. It's no big deal. He questioned me, too, so what?" Mark said without emotion.

"He practically accused me of burning your barn down and almost killing your stupid horses, that's what."

"Well, did you?"

"WHAT?" she yelled.

"Did you set my barn on fire and almost kill my horses?"

"How dare you ask me such a question. I should have my father sue you."

"Go ahead. It still won't change anything between us."

"Because of you, I had to have my father come home from his office so I was represented by an attorney when the Fire Marshall questioned me," she said angrily.

"If you had nothing to hide, what did you need an attorney for? For that matter, what did you need daddy for? You're an adult, remember?"

"I needed him to protect my rights, of course. This is all because of you," she insisted.

"Because of me someone burned my barn down. Because of me, you had to answer a few questions from the Fire Marshall. Because of me you couldn't have your damn party tonight. Well, isn't that just too damn bad," Mark said without raising his voice.

"Do you hate me that much?" she asked.

"No, I don't hate you at all. You are just a spoiled brat that has never had to grow up. Now I have better things to do than waste my time listening to you whine," Mark said, as he grew more impatient with her.

"What are you going to do about it," she asked, her voice having become softer and more childlike.

"About what?"

"About the Fire Marshall."

"Nothing. He has a job to do. All I did was answer his questions honestly. He asked me if there was anyone who was angry or upset with me. I told him that you were over our breaking up. I never suggested you started the fire. Now if that is all you have to say, then this conversation is over," Mark said then hung up the phone without giving her the chance to say anything more.

Mark stood for a second or two just looking at the phone. He almost expected her to call him back and yell at him some more, but the phone did not ring.

When Mark was reasonably certain she was not going to call him back, he fixed himself something to eat and then went into the living room and turned on the television so he could watch the news. When the news was over, he went into the bathroom. He took a shower and got ready for bed.

As he got into bed, Casey jumped up on the bed and laid down beside him. He reached down and gently rubbed Casey's ears.

"You're a good companion," he said, then laid his head on the pillow and closed his eyes.

CHAPTER FOURTEEN

During the week that followed Lora coming to the ranch, Mark didn't try to contact her. To his way of thinking she had made it clear she didn't want to see him. He had seen a small car go up the road to her ranch house on several occasions, but didn't see who it was. He felt it was none of his business. He guessed it was most likely one of Lora's friends who was getting her the things she would need.

The Fire Marshall had come by after a couple of days and told Mark that he could clear away the remains of his old barn. He was finished with the onsite part of his investigation. Mark called a company in Denver who did that kind of work. They came out and cleared it away.

Mark spent most of his time contacting construction companies to get bids on a new barn. The one saving factor, as far as he was concerned, was he still had the plans used to build the original barn. He didn't have to take the time to have a new set of plans drawn up.

During the time Mark was working on lining up someone to build his new barn, he had seen Lora sitting on the rear deck of her house on a couple of occasions. She appeared to be enjoying the sunshine and nice weather. He had to admit he had thought about going up to see her, but he would quickly remember she had told him to leave. He also remembered he had resolved not to go see her unless she invited him.

A week had gone by since the Fire Marshall had told Mark he could clear the remains of his barn away. A construction crew had arrived early that morning and had already started to build his new barn.

Mark was out in the pasture working with one of his horses. He rode up close to where the crew was working and stopped. He signaled to the foreman that he would like to speak to him. The foreman came over to talk to Mark.

"How's it going?" Mark asked.

"Pretty good. This is a rather simple plan. It shouldn't take us very long to put this building up and have it ready for use within a week or so if the weather cooperates."

"Did you notice the change on the back wall of the building?" Mark asked.

"Yes, I did. It's no problem to put in a door without a window."

"I still want the door, just not the window."

"I understand," the foreman said with a smile and a nod.

"Good. I'll be gone for a little while. I left some pop and lemonade in the cooler on the porch. If any of you would like something to drink feel free to help yourself. I don't have any beer right now."

"That's okay. I don't allow my crew to have any alcohol on the job, but we appreciate the pop and lemonade. Thank you, Mr. Howard."

Mark nodded briefly, then turned his horse and rode off across the pasture. He was headed for a trail on the U.S. Forest Service land bordering his property. The trail just inside the U.S. Forest Service land ran along the back fence of Lora's ranch, too.

As Mark rode along, he glanced up toward the back porch of Lora's ranch house. He could see her sitting on a lounger. There was no one else around that he could see. It didn't look as if Lora was looking toward him so he continued on his way.

It was always a pleasant ride in the forest, Mark thought. He would have preferred to share his time with someone on such a nice day; but if Lora didn't want to see him, he would enjoy the day by himself.

Lora was reclining on her lounger enjoying the sun when a woman about Lora's age came out of the house with a glass of iced tea in each hand. The woman put the glasses down on a table next to the lounger, pulled up a chair and sat down.

The young woman was Kim Becker, one of the women Lora worked with and her best friend. Kim was tall and slim with long dark brown hair and deep brown eyes. She had a pleasant smile and a devilish grin. She liked to wear clothes that were a little on the tight side and that tended to show off her very nice figure. There was no doubt Kim looked good in her skintight jeans. She was somewhat of a flirt and that gave her a reputation of being a little bit easy, although Lora knew better.

"Who's the cowboy?" Kim said as she reached for her glass of tea.

"What?" Lora replied, not sure what her friend was talking about.

"I saw some guy in a cowboy hat riding a horse on the other side of the fence. From what I could see of him, he was a nice looking guy," she said with a smile.

"Oh, that's probably my neighbor," Lora replied casually.

"I wouldn't mind going riding in the woods with him. Is he the guy you told me about?"

"I didn't see who it was, but it was probably Mark Howard. He often rides on the U.S. Forest Service land."

"Is he the same guy who saved you?"

"Yes, he is," Lora admitted reluctantly.

"Wow. Not only handsome, but a real knight in shining armor. How lucky for you."

"I don't know. He was nice to me. I'll admit that," she said, her voice showing hints of sadness.

"Damn, girl, are you blind? He's one sexy looking guy. Does he have a white horse?"

"I don't know, but he might," Lora said shaking her head.

"Is he single?"

"Yes."

"He's single, he's gallant and he's handsome, and you haven't made a play for him? What is wrong with you? You could have had him over here all this time taking care of all your needs, and I'm not just referring to helping you because of your injuries," Kim said with a devilish grin.

"I'm sure he has a life of his own. He doesn't need me tying him down."

"Why aren't you trying to make yourself part of his life?"

"I've had about enough of men for awhile," she said sharply, but not really believing what she said.

"Oh. Just because you happen to get a bad one, then I suppose you think they are all alike. Well, I've got news for you, honey, they're as different as night and day. It just takes a little work sometimes to separate the good ones from the bad ones. Sometimes you get lucky and happen to stumble onto a good one the first time," Kim said as if she were a woman of the world.

"I don't see you with the "right" man. If you're so smart, why aren't you married and raising a family by now?" Lora asked sarcastically.

"I haven't been looking, but if you're not going after this dreamboat, then I think I might like to meet him," Kim said.

"Well, you can have him," Lora said. "He lives just down the road. But if you just can't wait to meet him, why don't you stroll on down by the fence and wait for him. He'll be back in about two hours," Lora said, the tone of her voice showing that she was not interested in carrying on any more of their conversation about Mark.

It was clear to Kim that Lora must have been watching Mark fairly closely. How else would she know how long he would be gone if she hadn't been?

"Two hours, huh?" Kim asked as she looked at Lora.

"Yes," she replied, the tone of her voice showing she might be having second thoughts about giving Kim so much information.

"I just might go down there and talk to him," Kim said, as she looked over the top of her glass at Lora.

"Knock yourself out," Lora said, but she wasn't sure she really meant it.

Lora didn't look at Kim. Instead, she looked down at her glass of tea. She wasn't sure what it was that made her feel like she had given something away she really wanted to keep, especially since she really never had him to keep in the first place.

There was no doubt in her mind Mark was handsome and that he was kind. He had done nothing to her that would indicate he was anything other than what he had presented himself to be. But with her unpleasant experiences with men, she was afraid to find out, afraid of getting hurt again.

Now she had opened the door for Kim to pursue Mark, and she was beginning to question her own thinking. What if Kim was right?

Giving it some thought, Lora realized Kim was probably right. Deep down she had known it all along. Men were no more alike than women were alike. Lora had known other women who had loving and devoted husbands who would no more consider doing anything that would cause a riff in their marriages than they would to shoot themselves.

"You did say about two hours, didn't you?" Kim asked, rubbing it in a bit.

Lora almost jumped at the sound of Kim's question. She had been so deep in thought it had startled her. Lora looked over at Kim.

"Yes. Yes, I did," she replied reluctantly.

For the next hour neither of them said much of anything. Lora sat on the lounger and thought about Mark as she sipped on her iced tea.

Kim was not thinking about Mark. She was thinking about her friend, Lora. It was clear the men in Lora's life had been down right obnoxious and nasty. It was time for her to get Lora to see that there were good men out there, too. She wasn't sure how she was going to go about it, but it wouldn't hurt if she could find out how Mark felt about Lora. If he liked her or was at least a little interested in Lora, maybe she could find a way to get them together.

When a little over an hour had passed, Kim decided it was time for her to take a walk down to the fence. If Mark came along as Lora said he would, she would try to start a conversation with him. She liked horses and had ridden them. She felt it would be a good place to start.

"I guess I'll take a walk," Kim said as she stood up.

Lora watched Kim as she turned and walked off the pouch. At first she wasn't sure where Kim was going. But when Kim started off across the field toward the fence, she had to wonder if Kim really was going to try to meet Mark.

"Where are you going?" Lora asked.

"Oh, just down to the fence," Kim said as she looked back over her shoulder and smiled.

Lora watched Kim walk toward the fence. She noticed Kim had a little bounce in her step. It was hard for Lora to believe Kim was going to throw herself at Mark.

As Kim walked across the pasture to the fence that separated Lora's ranch from the U.S. Forest Service land, she wanted to turn around and see the look on Lora's face. But to do that would ruin everything. Lora would know she was doing it to make her jealous.

When Kim got to the fence, she stopped and casually leaned against one of the fence posts. She looked out into the forest but she did not see anyone. Kim began to wonder how long she would have to wait before Mark might show up. If he didn't show up, it would open the door for Lora to give her a hard time about throwing herself at a complete stranger. But on the other hand if it worked, it might open Lora's eyes.

Suddenly Kim heard a branch crack. She looked in the direction of the sound and saw a man on a horse coming out of the woods on the narrow trail that ran along the fence. Kim watched Mark as he came closer.

This was the first good look she got of Mark. Kim sort of smiled to herself when she realized he was as handsome as she had thought. She was impressed at how well he sat a horse and how at ease he was on the big animal.

Mark saw the woman standing next to the fence. He wondered who she was. As he moved closer, he got the feeling she might want to talk to him.

"Howdy, cowboy," Kim called out with a big smile.

ark didn't miss the fact she had a very sexy smile and she looked good in tight jeans.

"Howdy, Ma'am," Mark replied as he reached up and touched the brim of his cowboy hat.

"That's a nice looking horse, you've got there."

"He's a good horse," Mark said as he reined up next to the fence. "You a friend of Lora's?"

"Yes. We've been friends for a good number of years."

"How's she getting along?"

"Oh, fine. She doesn't need the wheelchair any more, but she still uses a walker. She has to be careful. Her wrist is doing real well, too. She really doesn't need much help any more."

"That's good," Mark replied as he glanced up toward the house.

Mark's horse moved up a little closer to the fence and put his head over it. Mark watched as Kim reached out and put her hand on the horse's nose. The horse raised his head just briefly, then tipped his head back down to let her rub the bridge of his nose.

"Your horse seems friendly enough."

"He's a good animal. Do you ride?"

"I have and I like to, but I don't get the chance very often," Kim replied as she looked up at Mark.

"You're welcome to come over sometime for a ride if you like. I have another horse."

"Is that an invitation?" Kim asked smiling up at him.

"It is," he replied as he smiled back at her.

"That would be nice. When would it be convenient for you?"

"I have to check on the work on my barn, but I do need to exercise my other horse. How about in an hour?"

"About an hour would be fine."

"I live right over there," he said as he pointed toward his house.

"I'll see you in about an hour," Kim said with a smile.

"Great," Mark said as he reached up and touched the brim of his hat.

Kim nodded and smiled back at him as he reined his horse back away from the fence. Mark nudged the horse gently in the ribs. The horse quickly trotted off down the trail toward home.

Kim stood at the fence and watched as Mark rode off. As she turned around, she could see Lora watching her. She wasn't sure what was going on in Lora's head, but from the look on her face she was not very happy. It would serve her right if I took him away from her, Kim thought as she walked across the pasture.

Kim was surprised at her last thought. It had not been her intention to take Mark away from Lora, only to make her see she really wanted to get to know Mark.

Mark was the first man that had caught Kim's attention so quickly. She had found him not only handsome, but he was friendly. He seemed to have a good personality, the thing Kim wanted most in a man.

When Kim stepped back onto the porch, the expression on Lora's face was one of disbelief and disappointment. Lora was looking at Kim.

"What?" Kim asked as if she had no idea what Lora was thinking.

"I can't believe you did that?"

"Did what?"

"Threw yourself at him like that," Lora said angrily.

"Hey, wait a minute. You're the one that said I could have him," Kim retorted. "Besides, I didn't throw myself at him. He simply invited me to go for a ride with him. I'm going over there and go for a ride with him."

"Some friend you turned out to be," Lora said.

"Listen, you made it clear you wanted nothing to do with him. I don't know if he's right for me or not, but I'm not afraid to find out," Kim retorted.

"And I am?"

"As a matter of fact, yes. Just how long are you going to sit around here feeling sorry for yourself? Just because you got burned doesn't give you the right to put every single male in the same category as that arrogant ass you were so hung up on. I knew he wasn't right for you from the very beginning. Even a blind person could have seen that."

"Why didn't you say something?" Lora said angrily.

"Let me ask you this. Would you have listened?" Kim asked as she looked Lora square in the eyes.

Lora looked back at her friend. It slowly began to sink in that her dearest friend was being totally honest with her. It was something she had not done for herself. She knew she would not have listened. She also knew Kim was right. It was way past time to develop a little backbone and put the past behind her where it belonged. She was scheduled to get the soft casts off her ankle and wrist tomorrow. She would go back to work on Monday and start her life over.

"You're right," Lora admitted. "You go and have a good time this afternoon. I have a lot of things to think about, and I think it would be best if I was alone for a little while."

"You sure? I can cancel the ride if you want to talk," Kim said, feeling a little sorry that she had been so blunt.

"No. You go and have a good time. I'll see you when you get back," Lora insisted.

With that said, Lora stood up and went into the house. Kim sat out on the porch to think. When it was time to go for the horseback ride, Kim stood up and walked to Mark's ranch.

CHAPTER FIFTEEN

As Kim came around the corner of Mark's storage shed, she saw Mark saddling his other horse. The horse he had been riding earlier was tied to a nearby fence post. She watched Mark as he tossed a saddle blanket over the horse's back and smoothed it out. He then tossed the heavy Western saddle onto the horse's back with very little effort.

Kim got a good chance to look Mark over while he worked. He was tall and handsome with broad shoulders and narrow waist. It didn't slip by her that his jeans fit him well. It was clear to Kim that he was strong' and it probably had not been very difficult for him to carry Lora to the house after her accident. It was not difficult for her to see why Lora liked him, even though she would not admit it.

Just as Mark finished tightening the cinch, Kim decided it was time to let him know she was there. She stepped out from behind the corner of the storage shed and walked toward him.

"Hi. Is that the horse I get to ride," she asked with a grin as she walked toward Mark.

Mark turned around and smiled. He noticed she had a slight bounce in her step. Mark gave her a quick once over. She still had on the skin-tight jeans and a nice fitting blouse that showed off her full figure very nicely.

"It sure is. Would you like to hop up in the saddle so I can adjust the stirrups?"

"I don't know about hopping up in the saddle, but I will certainly get in the saddle, that is if you will give me a hand," she said with a twinkle in her eyes.

Kim stepped up to the horse and took hold of the saddle horn. As she raised her foot, Mark helped her guide her foot into the stirrup. She swung herself into the saddle and sat down with the ease of someone who had ridden before. She looked down at Mark and watched him as he adjusted the stirrups.

"There you go, all set for a ride," he said looking up at her as he handed her the reins.

"It's been some time since I've been in the saddle."

"You don't look like it. Besides, Margo will understand. She's about as gentle a horse as they come, but she's not one bit shy about running. She's used to having different people on her."

"Margo? Her name's Margo?" Kim said with a surprised look on her face.

"My mother named her," Mark replied as he walked over and untied his horse. "Her sister's name was Margo, at least that was what they called her."

"I'm not sure I would like a horse named after me," Kim said as she patted the horse on the neck.

"My mother said my horse had the same temperament as my Aunt Margo had," Mark said as he swung into the saddle and then looked over his shoulder at Kim to see if she was ready.

Mark nudged his horse in the sides and started off toward the U.S. Forest Service land. Kim nudged Margo in the sides and the horse quickly trotted up beside Mark's horse.

"I'm almost afraid to ask what your horse's name is," Kim said once she was riding beside him.

"Sparky."

"Sparky? That has got to be good story," Kim said with a chuckle.

"When he was a colt he chewed through an electric wire in the barn at my father's ranch. It sparked before it blew the fuse. He jumped around and ran off across the field. It had to have hurt because it burned his mouth. My father started calling him Sparky and somehow the name seemed to stick. Oh, by the way, he doesn't chew on wires any more."

"I'll bet not."

"He's a good horse though. He's got heart and he can run," Mark said proudly.

As they came around from behind a row of trees to the place in the trail that wandered along the fence at the back of Lora's ranch, Mark looked up toward the house. His mind drifted off to thoughts of Lora. Although Kim seemed nice enough and she was certainly a very pretty woman, even sexy, it was Lora that held Mark's interest.

Mark knew Lora had a lot to deal with. She had just ended a bad relationship that had hurt her deeply and she was apparently not ready to try again. He could understand that. After all, he had just ended a bad relationship himself, but his was different. He had known for some time that it wasn't working out.

As they rode along the fence, Mark didn't see Lora on the porch. He thought he could see someone looking out the patio window. It was a good distance away and there was a bit of glare on the window so he couldn't be sure. He would have liked it if Lora was the one riding with him, but she had chosen to send him away.

"She's watching us from the window, you know," Kim said.

"What?" Mark asked as he swung around to look at Kim.

"I said she's watching us. She's in the window."

Mark could see the look in Kim's eyes. He was sure she was disappointed that he seemed more interested in Lora than in her.

"I'm sorry," Mark said.

"That's okay. I know you care about her. I also know she cares about you."

"Well, she has a strange way of showing it."

Mark just looked at her as the horses continued to walk along the trail. He wasn't sure what she was getting at, but he got the feeling she understood.

"I'm sorry. It's not right that I should be here with you and thinking about her," Mark said softly.

"Hey, don't let it bother you. I invited myself for this ride. You didn't promise me anything. Actually, I came for a ride with you for two reasons," she said sheepishly.

"Oh, really? What are the reasons?"

"Lora likes you. She likes you a lot," Kim started out.

"You'd never know it by the way she told me to leave."

"Maybe so, but she does. She's just afraid. She needs some time to work things out," Kim explained.

"You said you came on this ride for two reasons?"

"Yes. One is to find out how you really feel about Lora. And two, is to tell you how she feels about you."

"How does she feel about me?"

"I think she's in love with you."

"Yeah, sure. If she's so darn much in love with me, why did she run me off?"

"That's the hard part," Kim admitted.

"Hard for who?"

"For her, mostly, I think, but maybe for you, too. I'm not sure she knows that she is in love with you."

"That certainly makes it hard all right."

"You don't understand."

"You've got that right," Mark admitted.

"You see, she wants you around, but she is afraid you will be like Bowman."

"But I'm not like Bowman."

"I know that and so does she. But she's not ready to take the risk to find out who you really are."

"Great. She does and she doesn't," Mark said cynically.

"Right. Now it's up to you to win her over."

"And how am I supposed to do that? This Bowman fella sent her a big bouquet of roses and it didn't do him any good."

"It won't do you any good, either. She's not looking for someone who can send her things or spend a lot of money on her. She's looking for someone who will treat her right. Anyone can send her flowers, but it takes time and effort to give her a chance to get to know you."

"What you're saying is I need to let her know who I am and what kind of a person I am, rather than what I can spend on her. Is that what I'm hearing?" Mark asked.

"You're getting it," Kim said with a smile.

"This could take some time."

"That's just it. You have to take your time. You shouldn't be at her beck and call any and every time she wants you. You should have things you do she is not involved in. You should invite her to share in some of the things you do, but not all," Kim explained. "Do you get what I mean?"

"I think so."

"You should not insist on doing everything she likes, either. She needs to know you trust her enough to let her do things without you. One of the things Bowman did that should have sent a signal to Lora that their relationship was not on good solid ground was Bowman always wanted her at his beck and call. No one should be at anyone's beck and call. He also didn't like her going places without him."

"I get it," Mark said thoughtfully. "I shouldn't jump at every one of her whims any more then I should expect her to jump at mine."

"Right, but above all if you tell her you love her, you have to be loyal. No woman, or man, likes the person she loves to be unfaithful. Loyalty is everything in a relationship."

"I know that, but how do I get her to believe I will be loyal?"

"Only time will show her. There is no way to prove you will be loyal instantly."

Mark looked at Kim. He understood everything she was saying. He had been hurt by a failed relationship before and he knew how long it took him to get over it. He also knew his relationship with Barbara was all Barbara. He was a convenience to her. What she thought was love was her self-centeredness. As long as she was happy and getting her way, she considered herself in love.

"Just where do you think I should start?" Mark asked.

"Lora gets her casts off tomorrow morning. Why don't you stop over after lunch and ask her if she would like to go out to dinner to celebrate the freedom of no casts?"

"Good idea, but what makes you sure she will return to her ranch once her casts are off?"

"Don't worry about that. I'll make sure she's here at lunch time," Kim said with a smile.

Mark thought about what Kim was planning. He didn't like to pull surprises on people and he didn't like people trying to fix him up with someone. But in this case he would make an exception, reluctantly.

Once he was satisfied that things might be headed in the right direction, he took a look around. They had been talking and the horses had been walking. They had gone well down the trail and he hadn't even noticed how far they had gone.

"Do you think it's time to head back?" Mark asked. "I wouldn't want Lora to get the wrong idea about us."

"She already has the wrong idea about us, but I will get her straightened out," Kim said with a grin.

Mark smiled and turned his horse around to start back. As Kim rode up along side him, he wondered how Lora was feeling about him riding off with Kim. It didn't seem to him to be the best way to start a relationship, or the best way for him to show her that he was loyal to her. But then, she had been the one to send him away.

Mark glanced over at Kim. She was nice enough and she was a good looking woman. To Mark, that was enough to make some women jealous. He had to wonder if making Lora jealous with the way she was feeling now was such a good idea.

Kim watched Mark out of the corner of her eye as they rode along. She wondered what he was thinking. It was clear his interest was in Lora and not her, although she wouldn't mind if he had taken an interest in her. He was a nice guy. She even liked him, but he was not interested in her and that was the difference. If he had been interested in her, she might not have been so willing to help him get to know Lora better.

When they got to the fence at the back of Lora's property, Kim reined up Margo. She sat on the horse and looked at Mark.

"I think I'll get off here and go up to the house if you don't mind."

"Okay. Thanks for going with me," Mark said.

"It will all work out. You wait and see."

Mark looked up at the house. He wasn't so sure.

"I hope so," he said as he watched Kim get off the horse.

Kim handed the reins to Mark as she looked up him.

"If it doesn't work out, I'm currently available. But I wouldn't wait too long if I were you," she said with a smile.

"I'll keep that in mind," he replied with a smile.

Kim looked up at him for a few seconds, then she turned and stepped through the fence. Mark watched her as she walked away, then looked up at the house. He wondered if Lora was watching them from the window. It really didn't matter if she was watching him. If she was not interested in him, he would know soon enough.

He turned his horse away and headed off for his ranch. When he got back to the ranch he rode over to the storage shed. He took the saddles off the horses and put them in the storage shed. He gave each of the horses a rub down and removed their bridles. He then turned them loose in the pasture. He would come out and feed them later.

As he walked toward the house, he noticed the building crew had done a lot since he left. It would not take long to have a new barn at this rate, he thought.

Once inside the house, he fixed his dinner and sat down to watch a bit of news while he ate. He found it hard to concentrate on the news as he thought of Kim's plan to get Lora to be more receptive to him. He didn't know if it would work and he wasn't all that excited about it. He had this feeling it was being a little deceptive, and he didn't like that idea. But on the other hand, he didn't have a better idea at the moment.

It was getting late and he was tired. After he fed his dog and cleaned up the kitchen, he went out and took care of the horses.

When he returned to the house, he decided it was time to turn in. He took a shower and got ready for bed. Mark was in bed earlier than usual, but it had been a long week. A lot had happened and he had a lot to think about.

Sleep didn't come easy as his mind was cluttered with a lot of random thoughts.

Morning came early for Mark. He had spent most of the night tossing and turning. Kim's plan to get him back in the good graces of Lora hadn't set well with him. He didn't like deceiving people, and that was how he saw Kim's plan.

Since he was not getting any sleep, he decided he might as well get up and get started on his day. As soon as he had gotten dressed, he went out to the kitchen and fixed himself breakfast. After feeding Casey, he went outside to feed and take care of his horses.

On his way out to the pasture where he had left his horses he noticed the crew building the new barn was already hard at work and the progress was going well. He stopped and visited with the crew for a few minutes before going on out to the pasture.

It took him a few minutes to get his horses attention as they were on the far side of the pasture enjoying the moist green grass. Once he finally got them to come to him, he fed them some hay and a bit of grain before returning to the house.

When he returned to the house, he noticed a car coming down the driveway. It was a car he didn't recognize so he stopped and waited to see who it was. When the car turned and stopped in front of the house, he was able to see who was driving it. It was Lora. He was surprised to see her. He didn't know that she had a car or that she was driving yet.

As soon as the car stopped, he walked over to the car. He watched it as he approached. He didn't know if she had gotten a new car, but it looked pretty nice.

"Hi. Nice car," he said smiling as he leaned against it and looked inside. "Good to see you out and about."

"Hi. It's good to be out and about," she replied softly without further comment and then turned and looked out the windshield.

Mark wondered what was on her mind after all she had come to his ranch. The look on her face gave him the impression she was trying to get her thoughts together. It quickly became obvious to him that she had not come to show off her new car.

"Is there something wrong?" Mark asked.

She turned and looked up at him. Lora didn't like looking into his eyes as she could see his concern for her in them. It tended to make her feel a little uncomfortable and even a little guilty for sending him away like she had. After all, he was the reason she was here at all.

"I'm on my way into town to get my casts off."

"That's great, but I thought Kim was going to take you," he said.

"She was, but as you can see I'm quite capable of driving myself."

"I can see that and it's great," Mark replied.

"I . . . ah . . . . I just wanted to tell you not to come up to the house later this morning to ask me out for dinner," she said and then turned to look out the windshield again.

Mark quickly realized Kim must have told her about her plan to get them together. It was obvious she didn't like Kim's plan, but he wasn't crazy about it, either.

"May I ask why?"

"Because I don't want to go out with you," she said, unable to look him in the eyes when she said it.

Her statement caught Mark off guard. He didn't know what was going on, but he needed to know what sort of a problem she had with him.

"Why? Are you afraid you might find out I'm a lot different from Jeff? Are you afraid you might just find out you like me?" Mark asked, obviously a little upset with her for turning him away without even giving herself a chance.

Lora looked at him, her eyes narrow. She was upset with him. It was clear in the way she looked at him.

"I don't like it when someone tries to play matchmaker behind my back," she said sharply.

"I don't like it, either," he said responding almost as sharply as she had. "For your information, it wasn't my idea in the first place."

"I suppose it was Kim's idea?"

"Yes, as a matter of fact it was. Look, I've been doing what you asked. You told me to go away and I left. I have not once come knocking at your door. Now I would like to call on you, but if that's too much for you to handle and you really don't want me to, all you have to do is say so and I won't bother you again," Mark said with an underlying tone of anger in his voice and a feeling of frustration with her.

Mark stepped back away from the car and looked at her as he waited for an answer from her. He hoped she would say he could come see her, but he didn't really expect it to happen. In fact, the way the conversation had been going, he was beginning to think maybe he didn't want to call on her after all. If it was going to be like this all the time then why bother, he thought.

"If you would like to stop over for coffee some afternoon, I guess it would be okay. I have to go now," she said softly, almost as if she was giving in when she really didn't want to.

"We'll see," he said as he stepped back further away from the car.

Mark stood in front of his house and watched as Lora drove away. He took a deep breath and thought about what she had said. The thought passed through his mind that if it was that much trouble for her to even let him visit her, maybe it wasn't worth his trouble.

After all, there was no sense in getting rejected again and again.

As the car disappeared from sight, Mark thought about what had just happened. He decided he would have to think about it for a day or so. From the way she had talked, she didn't sound as if she even cared one way or the other if he visited with her or not. Maybe he shouldn't care, either.

CHAPTER SIXTEEN

As Lora drove back down the driveway, she glanced in her rearview mirror at Mark standing there watching her drive away. She wasn't sure if she had done the right thing by telling him he could stop in for coffee. She knew deep down in her heart that he was different from Jeff. The only question was he different enough? She wasn't sure if she had the courage to find out.

It wasn't long before she was on the Interstate headed toward Denver. She went directly to her doctor's office to have the casts removed. Since she was his first patient of the day, it took her only about an hour at the doctor's office. He had given her a clean bill of health and told her that she could do almost anything she wanted as long as she didn't over do it. If she got tired or she started to have pain in her ankle or wrist, she should stop and rest.

Lora was glad she no longer had to have the casts. She was also glad she was able to get a car on loan, paid for by her insurance company. But she also needed to get her life back to some type of normalcy as soon as possible.

While she was in town, she had several stops to make. During the time she was laid up, she had had time to think about what she needed to do as soon as she got her casts off. She had decided she didn't need to have two places. Since the ranch was free and clear of any debt, she made the decision to take a few more days off from work and get herself moved up to the ranch before returning to work. At least that way she would not have to pay rent on her town house.

The other thing she needed to do was to get a new vehicle. That was another thing she had had plenty of time to think about as well as to plan for. Since she had made the decision to live at the ranch, she felt it might be a good idea if she bought herself a four-wheel drive vehicle.

If she was going to move over the next few days, she felt the first thing she should do was to get the new vehicle so she could use it to move her personal belongings, and return the rented car.

Lora went to her town house and sat down at her computer. She looked up different kinds of SUV's on it and picked out a Dodge Durango. She even checked out prices. Since she had money in the bank from her grandfather and she had the money from the insurance company, she could pay cash for it.

She spent the rest of the morning getting money transferred to her checking account and then went to lunch. After lunch she went to a Dodge dealer and picked out the Durango she wanted. The salesman had tried to get a better price for the Durango, but she had a copy of what the car cost the dealer and had already decided on how much she was willing to pay for it. It wasn't until she turned and started out the door that the salesman finally accepted her offer for the Durango. She had to smile to herself after signing the papers since she had gotten what she felt was a good deal.

It didn't take them long to have her new vehicle ready for her to drive away in. She walked out of the showroom and into her brand new bright red Dodge Durango. Lora turned the key and headed for her town house. Before she left the dealership, she had

called the car rental place and made
arrangements for one of their people to pick
up the rental car at the dealership.

When she got to her town house, she
began to pack up her belongings. She began
to realize how much she had to move. She
also realized she was going to need help
moving it.

She thought of Mark and how she had
treated him. There was no way she could ask
him for his help now. The more she thought
about it, the more she realized that if she
asked him to help her after the way she had
treated him, she would be using him. If she
did that, she would be no different than Jeff,
someone who uses others to get what they
want.

Lora picked up the phone book and called
a couple of moving companies that did local
moves. She lined one up to come the next
morning to pack up her things and move them
to the ranch house. After the arrangements
were made, she felt better. She was being the
independent woman she had always thought
herself to be.

She loaded some of her valuables in her
new car and got ready to drive back to the

ranch house. As she drove back to the ranch house, she began to wonder if Mark would come over and "call" on her.

She began to realize her last conversation with him had not been one that would encourage him to call on her. She had not been at all fair with him. The more she thought about it, the more she believed it had to have been Kim's idea to get them together. He had done so much for her already, and she had repaid him by being anything but friendly toward him. She had done just about everything she could to discourage him without coming right out and telling him that she never wanted to see him.

It was at that moment she remembered the one lonely little yellow rose he had gotten her when she was in the hospital. She knew that a yellow rose was a sign of friendship. Lora wondered if Mark knew what a yellow rose meant. If he did, then all he seemed to want was to be friends.

The thought occurred to her to give him a chance to become her friend, if it wasn't already too late. If anything came of it, then that would be all right. If they remained just friends, then that was the way it was supposed to be.

Maybe Kim had been right. It began to soak into her mind that if she didn't take the risk to get to know Mark, she might lose the one person she could truly love and who would truly love her.

As she drove past the drive to Mark's ranch, she thought for a moment that she might like to turn in, apologize to him and invite him over for coffee when the movers come tomorrow. She quickly decided against it because he might look at it as more than just coffee. He might think she was asking him over so she wouldn't have to be alone with the movers.

Lora drove on home and parked her new car in front of the garage. It was getting on toward dinnertime when she got to the ranch house. She unloaded her car. When she was finished, she went inside and began to fix herself some dinner.

As Lora prepared her dinner, the thought of Mark crossed her mind again. She wondered what it was he liked to eat. Was he a meat and potatoes sort of guy, or did he like salads and steak? Was he into stir-fries, or did he prefer fish?

After she had finished her dinner and was cleaning up the kitchen, she found she could not get Mark off her mind. It started to become very clear she really didn't know very much about him. In fact, she knew nothing at all about him except he had gone out of his way to be helpful. It occurred to her that she really did want to know about him, what he liked, what he didn't like, and what he was like as a person. It also occurred to her that because of the way she had talked to him, she might not get the chance to get to know him. She may have already burnt that bridge.

That thought reminded her that she knew his barn had burned down, but that was all she knew about it. The Fire Marshall had been there, but she had no idea what conclusion the Fire Marshall had come to with regard to the cause of the fire. Lora also knew about Mark's horses.

The fact his barn had burned down gave her an idea. She thought it would be a very neighborly gesture on her part to let him use her barn to put up his horses for the night until his new barn was finished.

Without thinking, she picked up the phone and called Mark. The phone rang several times before he answered. She began to wonder if he was at home, or if he had decided he just wasn't going to answer the phone. She was also beginning to wonder if it was such a good idea, but the phone was answered before she could change her mind.

"Hello?"

"Yes, is this Mark?"

"Yes."

"This is Lora Winters."

"Oh, hi," he said not sure what she was going to say to him this time. "I didn't expect you to call."

"I hope I'm not disturbing you, but I was thinking. I heard your barn had burned down. I was wondering if you are in need of a barn for your horses until you can get a new one built?"

"As a matter of fact, I could use a barn for a few days, maybe for as long as a week. I don't like to leave my horses out at night with the mountain lions we have living up here.

I've never had a problem with them, but I would prefer not to tempt them," he said.

"Well, I have an empty barn I'm not using. You are more than welcome to use it if you would like," she said her voice much more pleasant than it had been earlier in the day.

"Thank you, thank you so much. If you don't mind I will bring my horses over after dinner. I can assure you that I will keep your barn clean and I will pasture my horses over here."

"I'm sure you will take care of the barn, but you are more than welcome to let your horses graze over here. It would actually help keep the grass a little shorter."

"Thank you," Mark said, feeling a little better about her change in attitude.

"I don't think there is any hay in the barn so I'm afraid you would have to provide you own," she said, a tone of apology in her voice.

"That's no problem. If you don't mind I'll bring some hay over in my pickup."

"That would be fine," she agreed.

"Thank you, again."

"Ah, when you come over to put your horses up for the night, you are welcome to stop up at the house for a cup of coffee, if you would like."

"Ah . . yeah. I'd like that," Mark replied, wondering why the sudden change of heart.

"Just knock on the back patio door. I'll most likely be in the kitchen," she said.

"I will. I'll see you in about an hour and a half?"

"That would be fine. See you then," Lora said before hanging up.

Lora looked at the phone for a few minutes before she looked out toward the back porch. She caught a reflection of herself in the sliding glass patio door. She was smiling. It surprised her a little. It had been some time since she felt she had any reason to smile. She was actually looking forward to seeing Mark.

She looked around the kitchen and realized she had nothing for them to have with coffee. Lora remembered she had some canned pie filling, apple if she remembered correctly. It would make a good Apple Crunch. She went to work preparing and baking an Apple Crunch to share with Mark.

Mark had just finished dinner when Lora had called. As he hung up the phone, he wondered what might have caused her to change her attitude toward him. Had Kim gotten to her and convinced her to give him another chance? Maybe she was feeling indebted to him? He hoped that was not the reason for her change of heart. Maybe she had decided to simply be a good neighbor? That was it, he thought. She was just trying to be a good neighbor.

Lora had invited him to her place for coffee, and that was all he wanted in the first place, a chance to get to know her. He had no other motive for seeing her. He made the decision to go and have coffee with her, but he would be cautious and simply try to get to know her. But before he was ready to go visit her, he had work to do.

Mark went outside and got into his pickup. He drove it to the storage shed and loaded several bales of hay on it. As soon as it was loaded, he drove over to Lora's ranch and out to the barn.

As he pulled up in front of the barn, he looked up at the house. From the barn he could see Lora in the kitchen. Mark wasn't sure what she was doing, but it really didn't matter. He had been invited to come up to the house after he got his horses settled in the barn.

Mark stacked the hay in the barn, then returned home. He rounded up his horses and walked them up to Lora's barn. He tied his horses to the fence, then prepared a stall for each of them. He put out some grain and hay. Once the stalls were ready, he led his horses into the barn.

Now that his horses had been taken care of, he would go back to his place and clean up. There was no way to take care of horses and still remain clean.

As he walked back to his ranch house, he couldn't help but think of Lora. He was still wondering why she had a change of heart. Kim must have had a talk with Lora again and had explained that it had been her idea for him to "drop in" on her. That had to be it.

CHAPTER SEVENTEEN

When Mark came around the corner of his ranch house, his thoughts were disturbed by the sight of a car in the driveway. It was a black Lincoln Continental. At first he wasn't sure who it belonged to, but as he got closer he realized the car belonged to Frank Cooper, Barbara's father. Mark's first reaction was to turn around and leave before he was seen, but it was too late. Frank had seen him.

Frank had parked his car next to Mark's truck in front of the house. Not sure he wanted to hear what Frank had to say, Mark walked toward him.

"What do you want?" Mark asked with a sigh, wondering what else could go wrong today.

"My daughter is very upset with you," Frank said, but his voice was soft and reserved as if he wasn't happy about what was going on between Mark and his daughter.

"I'm sorry about that, but I really don't care. She is a spoiled brat. It's about time she learned she can't have everything she wants, the way she wants it."

"I agree with you, but it's a little more serious than that," Frank said.

Mark was surprised to hear Frank agree that Barbara was spoiled. The thing that caused him to wonder why he was here was his comment about it being more serious than that.

"You mind explaining?" Mark asked as he looked at Frank.

"Could we find a place to sit down where we can talk?" Frank asked, the look on his face indicating Mark might refuse.

"Sure. Come inside."

Mark led Frank into his house and motioned for him to sit down at the kitchen table. As Frank pulled up a chair to sit down, he looked around.

"This is a very nice place."

"Don't sound so surprised. I live like a lot of people."

"I'm sorry. I didn't mean for it to sound like I'm surprised you live in such a nice home. It's just that Barbara told me you live in a dinky little cabin in the woods with a hound and a couple of horses. Your home is not dinky. In fact, it is very nice. This is not at all what I had expected."

"Well, I do have a dog, but he's not a hound, he's a Lab. I do have two horses and I keep them in a very nice and modern barn, at least I did until someone decided to burn it down."

"Ah, yes. The barn."

Mark looked at him and wondered what that comment meant.

"It's the barn I wish to talk to you about," Frank continued.

"What about my barn?" Mark asked, curious as to why he would want to talk to him about his barn.

"I have come here to discuss your new barn."

"What about my new barn? And what does my barn have to do with you?"

Frank looked at Mark as if he wasn't sure how to say what was on his mind. Mark found it rather strange. He knew Frank to be a very good and self-assured attorney who always seemed to be able to talk even when he had nothing to say. The fact that he seemed to be unable to express himself caused Mark to wonder what was going on.

"It seems my daughter got a little upset with you the other day. In fact, she was darn right angry. She, ... ah . . . . ."

Frank stuttered and looked down at his hand. He was worried about what Mark might do once he explained why he was there.

"Let me guess. Barbara had one of her friends burn my barn down. Am I right?" Mark asked.

Frank looked at Mark. The expression on his face told Mark he hit the nail on the head.

"As a matter of fact, yes," he admitted reluctantly.

"It crossed my mind that she might have had something to do with it, but I found it difficult to believe she would go that far," Mark said as he shook his head in disbelief.

"She got scared when the State Fire Marshall came by the house and started asking her a lot of questions. It should have been a simple enough investigation with a few questions and that would be it. But when she called me and told me that she was being questioned and she had told the Fire Marshall she wanted a lawyer, I began to think she might have actually done it.

"After the Fire Marshall left, I started questioning her about it myself. She finally admitted that she had called one of her old boy friends, one I didn't like very well I might add, to burn your barn down. She even admitted that she told him that she didn't care if the horses were in the barn when he did it, but she wanted it done as quickly as possible," Frank explained.

Mark just sat there and looked at him. He could hardly believe what he had been told.

"Your daughter needs help," Mark said calmly.

"Yes, I know. I have protected her for years. Every time she got into trouble, I would get her out of it," he admitted.

"Why did you come to talk to me? What is it you want?"

"I wanted to talk to you and see if there is some way we could come to an agreement and possibly a settlement without a lot of publicity."

"Even you have to admit she went too far this time. Once the State Fire Marshall got involved it was taken out of my hands."

"I know, but if you don't press charges it won't go so hard on her," he said, his eyes pleading for some understanding.

"What about my insurance company. They will go after her to get the money back it's costing them to rebuild my barn. I seriously doubt they will be so understanding."

"That's true, unless they get their money back without any hassle."

"Are you saying that you are going to pay for the new barn?"

"Yes. I would anyway. If I pay for it, I might be able to get the insurance company to back off."

"It's not going to be that easy to get the Fire Marshall to back off."

"I know," Frank said, then took a deep breath.

"What are you suggesting?"

"If she pleads guilty to hiring someone to burn down your barn, and you don't press charges, I might be able to get her off with probation. What do you say?"

"I don't know. It sounds to me like you're bailing her out again so she doesn't have to face the responsibility for what she has done. That's what you've been doing her whole life and look at her. You tell me, just what will she learn from that?" Mark asked.

Frank looked at him for a minute. His eyes were sad as if he knew he was going to have to make Barbara pay for her own mistakes.

Mark was sure it was not easy for Frank to harbor the idea that his little girl was probably going to go to jail. Although Mark didn't have any children, he knew it would hurt terribly to have to watch one of his children go to jail.

"I'll tell you what. Barbara caused a lot of expense to the state in the form of time and effort by the State Fire Marshal. There was also the time, equipment and manpower by the local fire department. That is to say nothing of the cost and expense of getting a new barn built.

"Now, if she reimburses all those expenses, admits to hiring someone to burn down my barn, and she gets some help for her psychological and emotional problems to help her face up to her responsibilities, I will consider dropping the charges.

"I also want your guarantee that she will not bother me again, ever, either in person, on the phone or by mail. And she will have to turn over the person she hired to burn down the barn so he can be charged," Mark said as he looked at Frank in the hope of seeing if Frank might agree to his demands.

Frank sat there and looked at Mark as he thought about the terms. There was no doubt in his mind that the conditions Mark offered were more than fair considering the circumstances. If he were in Mark's shoes, he would have demanded more.

Frank also knew his daughter would not be able to control her temper if she was put on the stand and cross-examined by a competent lawyer. He was sure she would probably end up convicting herself. At least this way, he might be able to keep Barbara out of jail.

"Will you push for jail time for Barbara at a sentencing hearing?" Frank asked.

"No. I don't really want to see her go to jail, but I do want her to get help."

"Okay. If you will get me the cost of the new barn and a list of all the expenses you have incurred as a result of Barbara's actions,

I will see to it you get paid for them in full. I will contact your insurance company and settle things with them. I will also put together everything we have agreed to in writing and bring it by for your approval," Frank said very business like.

"I make no promises about what the judge will do," Mark said. "Even if I don't file charges the judge may still insist on some jail time," Mark said.

"I know, but with our agreement, there is a good chance she will get off with probation and treatment to help her control her temper," Frank said.

Frank knew that he had a good deal for Barbara, and he knew he was dealing with a man who was not vengeful or spiteful. He also knew Mark expected the agreement to be carried out to the letter.

"That would be fine with me," Mark said. "But if all the terms of our agreement are not met, I can assure you that I will press charges. Do I make myself clear?"

"Yes. Very clear."

Frank and Mark stood up, their business completed for now. Frank reached across the table and stuck out his hand. Mark looked at it for a second then reached out to take his hand.

"I hope you hold no hard feelings toward my daughter," Frank said as he shook Mark's hand.

"No, I don't. I just think that she needs help."

Frank didn't say anything as he drew back his hand. However, he did nod in agreement with Mark.

Mark walked Frank to the door and watched him as he got into his car. He wondered how Barbara was going to take the news of what was required of her. Mark smiled to himself as he thought about how glad he was it was not his responsibility to tell her. There was no doubt in Mark's mind that when Frank presented the conditions of their agreement she would explode.

Mark took a quick look at his watch. It had been longer then he had told Lora it would take him to get his horses settled in her barn. If he was going to have coffee with her, he had better get a move on.

He hurried into his bathroom and took a quick shower. He decided he should wear some nice work clothes for his visit to Lora, as he didn't want her to think he was there for a "date". She had offered him coffee and that was all.

As soon as he was ready, he left his house with Casey at his side. He walked across the pasture toward Lora's ranch house. He made a quick stop at the barn to check and make sure his horses had settled into their new surroundings. They looked relaxed and didn't seem to mind their surroundings at all.

As he stepped out of the barn, he looked up at Lora's ranch house. He wondered if it was a good idea to go up to the house at this late hour. It had been over two hours since he had talked to Lora. If it had not been for Mr. Cooper stopping by, he would have been there earlier.

Mark decided he would go up and knock on the door. He would explain why he was later than he planned, and that he could stop over some other time for coffee if she thought it was too late.

He walked up to the back door and looked inside. Mark didn't see Lora in the kitchen, but the lights were still on. He reached out and knocked on the door, then waited. He was a little nervous that she might have gone to bed and she might not be too happy with him for being so late.

Lora heard the knock on the back door. As she headed out to the kitchen, she glanced at her watch. She wondered why it had taken Mark so long, but she was glad he had come by anyway.

"Hi," she said as she opened the door.

"I'm sorry I'm so late, but I had a last minute unexpected visitor. I hope it's not too late for coffee."

"No. It's fine. Please, come in," Lora said as she stepped back so Mark could enter.

"Stay," Mark said to Casey.

"Oh, it's all right if he comes in," Lora said as she smiled at Casey. "I like dogs as long as they're friendly."

"He's a good dog."

Mark stepped inside Lora's kitchen, then turned and motioned for Casey to come in and for Lora to shut the door. As she walked past Mark, she motioned toward the kitchen table.

"I made some Apple Crunch, would you like some with your coffee?"

"Sounds good, sure," Mark replied.

"How do you like your coffee?"

"Black, please."

Lora motioned for Mark to sit down at the table. She reached up and took a couple of cups out of the cupboard.

Mark watched her as she set the cups on the table, then poured the coffee. He watched her when she turned her back to him and started putting the Apple Crunch on plates. Mark found her to be very nice looking. He also found it hard to take his eyes off her.

When she turned back around and started toward the table, Mark smiled at her. She placed a serving of Apple Crunch in front of him.

"Can I get something for your dog?" Lora asked politely.

"No, he's already had his dinner," Mark replied as he glanced down at Casey lying on the floor next to the table.

Mark waited for Lora to sit down at the table. Once she was seated, Mark looked at the Apple Crunch then picked up the fork. He took a small portion of the crunch and put it in his mouth. All the time Lora watched him for his reaction. Mark savored the taste and smiled at her.

"This is very good," he said.

"It's a very simple recipe I got from my mother. She was a good cook."

"She should be proud of you," Mark said.

Lora turned a little red at Mark's remark. It embarrassed her to have someone compliment her. She wanted nothing more at the moment than to talk about something else.

"Did you get your horses settled in?"

"Yes. And thank you for the use of your barn."

"How are things going with the new barn?"

"Fine. It should be done in a few days, a week at the most, depending on the weather."

"That's good," she said, then took another sip of coffee.

Lora was having a hard time with him sitting across the table from her. She wanted to get to know him better, but she was a little afraid at the same time.

Mark wasn't sure how far this would go between them. He wasn't even sure how far he wanted it to go. There was no doubt in his mind that she was a pretty woman, he had seen that right off. He also knew she had a number of issues to deal with and there was a chance he was one of her issues.

"Was that your new car I saw you driving earlier?" he asked, not sure what to say.

"Oh. No. It was the car provided by the insurance company. I've already turned it back to them. I got a new car," she said with a hint of excitement in her voice.

"Oh, what did you get?"

"I bought a Dodge Durango," she said rather pleased with herself.

"Good SUV. I think you'll like it," he replied.

For some reason Lora could not understand, she found his approval of her choice of the SUV meant a good deal to her. She wasn't sure why it meant so much to her, but it did.

"When do you pick it up?"

"I already have it. Would you like to see it?" she asked not sure what he would think of the color.

"Sure," he replied as he took a sip of his coffee.

"It's out front."

Mark started to get up from the table, but stopped when she said with a smile, "You can finish your crunch first. It's not going anywhere."

Mark smiled and sat back down. While they finished eating, Lora told him about the salesman and how he tried to get her to pay more for it than she had decided it was worth to her.

"He didn't think I would walk off without it. I think he thought because I was a woman he could get more out of me. He found out when I set my mind to something, I can be pretty stubborn. I just turned and started out the door. It wasn't until he thought he was going to lose the deal that he realized he better sell it to me at the price I offered or he would lose out," she said with a grin.

"He probably thought you had your heart set on that particular Dodge, and you wouldn't walk away so easily. He should know there are several Dodge Dealers in the area and one of them would sell you what you want if he didn't," Mark said with a grin.

"You should have seen the look on his face when I just turned around and headed for the door," she said with a slight laugh.

Mark smiled, as he had not seen her laugh before. It was good to see she could laugh.

As soon as they had taken the last bite of crunch and swallowed the last of their coffee, they got up and started toward the front door. When they got to the door, Mark opened the door for her and followed her out to the driveway. Her new Dodge was sitting in the driveway right under the yard light.

"Wow, that's bright," he said with a grin.

"You think it's too bright?" Lora asked, worried he didn't like the color.

"No. I think it's pretty, like you," he said, then realized what he had said.

Lora looked up at him and smiled. She wasn't sure what to say, or if she should say anything. It was clear that the comment had come without any real thought.

"Thank you," she said shyly.

Mark was a little embarrassed by his comment. He wasn't sure what he should do so he turned and started to look over the SUV. He opened the door and looked inside to see all the bells and whistles it had. This one was loaded.

"Pretty nice. Pretty nice, indeed," Mark would say over and over as he looked over the SUV.

Lora watched him as he examined her new SUV. She couldn't help but smile to herself as she watched him check out all the gadgets. Lora found herself leaning close to him as he looked over the inside of the car.

Mark leaned back and started to turn around. He suddenly found himself only inches away from Lora. When he tried to avoid stumbling against her, he reached out and grabbed her in an effort to keep from knocking her over.

Lora wasn't sure just what had happened, but she suddenly found herself in Mark's arms. She was looking up at his face. Her reaction had been to grab hold of him in order to get her balance. They stood there for what seemed like time eternal while looking into each other's eyes.

When it finally soaked into Mark's consciousness that he was holding her in his arms, he took a deep breath and stepped back a little.

"I'm sorry. I didn't mean to almost knock you over. I didn't know you were standing that close to me," he said as he let go of her.

"It's okay," she said, her breath catching just a little.

Lora stepped back a little, took a deep breath, and then turned away. She had no idea what had come over her. Just the touch of Mark's hands on her had made her whole body aware of his closeness. It was as if an electric shock had gone through her entire body, but not one that caused her pain. Rather it was one that caused every nerve in her body to immediately come alive.

Mark was not unaware of what had happened, either. It had quickly passed through his mind that he wanted to kiss her. He could not figure out why he didn't, but he didn't. Something had just happened, but he had no idea what it was. All he knew was it felt good. The only thing he could think of at the moment was not to press his luck.

"Ah . . I ah, like your new car. It suits you," he said, hoping what he said made sense and he wasn't just babbling.

"Thank you," was all Lora could manage at the moment.

Mark turned around and looked at the car. He wasn't really seeing it as he was trying to get his thoughts together.

"You'll have to take me for a ride in it sometime," he said as he turned back around and looked into her eyes.

"Yes, I'll have to do that," she replied as she looked up at him.

Mark wasn't sure what to say, but he seemed to know it would be best if he ended this evening before he did something stupid. He wasn't sure what had happened up to now, but he needed some time to think about it.

"I want to thank you for the crunch and coffee, and of course, for showing me your new car, but I think I should go. I have a busy day tomorrow and it will start early."

"Yes, I understand. I have my things from town coming tomorrow. I should get some rest," she said.

"In that case, Goodnight," he said with a smile.

"Goodnight," Lora said, then turned and started for the house.

Mark watched and waited for her to go inside. As soon as she was safely in the house, he turned and walked around the house and out the back. He walked down past the barn and on across the pasture to his own ranch, all the time thinking about Lora.

Lora had gone into the house and shut the door behind her. She leaned back against the door and took in a deep breath. She still could not understand what had happened out there, but she did understand she wanted to see him again.

Realizing he had probably gone out the back to get home, she hurried to the back patio door and looked out. She caught a glimpse of him just before he disappeared in the darkness near the barn.

Lora continued to look at the place where she had last seen him. After several minutes, she let out a sigh and then went to her bedroom to get ready for bed. She laid in bed for a long time before she could get her mind to relax enough to allow her to get some sleep.

As soon as Mark got home, he got ready for bed. Sleep did not come easy for him. He could not get his mind to let go of the image of Lora looking up at him while he held her in his arms. Although she had been wrapped in his arms, the look in her eyes had been most unsettling for him. Only after a long period of restlessness did Mark finally fall asleep.

CHAPTER EIGHTEEN

When morning came Lora found herself wide awake long before she normally would even think about getting up. She had gone to sleep thinking about Mark and woke up with him on her mind. She got out of bed and went into the bathroom.

She immediately began to wonder what Mark might be doing. Was he still in bed, or was he up and at it already? It crossed her mind that it would have been nice if they could have breakfast together this morning, but that thought faded away quickly. She was sure he was probably hard at work taking care of his horses and most likely had had his breakfast already.

It was at that moment Lora remembered his horses were in her barn. She wondered if he might be working in the barn. She thought about it for a minute before she hurried back into her bedroom and grabbed her robe off the foot of the bed. She went out into the kitchen while still pulling her robe around her.

When she got to the back patio door, she looked out toward the barn. Mark's truck was nowhere in sight. She felt a little disappointed until it occurred to her that he might have simply walked over to the barn. After all, it wasn't very far and he had walked over last night. She looked out toward the pasture but didn't see his horses. He would have let the horses out if he was working in the barn, she thought. She quickly realized it was possible his horses were in her pasture, but in a part of the pasture hidden by the barn and the trees.

Her heart fluttered slightly as she thought he might not have come over yet to take care of his horses. She still might have time to get dressed and get down to the barn before he could get there. It would give her a chance to see him and to talk to him, maybe even help him clean the stalls.

She almost laughed out loud at the thought of cleaning stalls for someone else's horses. Cleaning out the stalls in a barn was one of those jobs no one liked to do, and here she was hoping he hadn't done it yet so she could help him. She shook her head as she thought about how it would look to him. It would be so obvious to even the dumbest of men that she was throwing herself at him.

"Do you really think it's such a good idea to throw yourself at him?" she asked herself out loud.

Just hearing her own question caused her to stop and think. She had just come off a disastrous relationship. Was she really ready to try to have a new relationship so soon? Her mind told her that she was not ready, but her heart told her that Mark could be the one man for her.

Lora made herself a cup of coffee and sat down at the kitchen table to think. She tried to think clearly and logically, but that was not easy because her heart contradicted everything her head told her.

Her head told her to step back and not to get too involved with him, to take it slow and easy until she knew him much better. The fact he was handsome, had an interesting life up here on the mountain, and seemed like a very nice man were not reasons enough to jump right back into a relationship.

On the other hand, her heart kept telling her that he was the right man, the one who would treat her the way she should be treated, with love, loyalty and respect. Lora found it hard to listen to her heart. She had been hurt too many times already. But on the other hand, maybe Kim was right. Maybe she was in love with him already.

Last night Mark had accidentally run into her. In order to keep her from falling and hurting herself, he grabbed hold of her. Lora could remember how her entire body felt when he had simply grabbed her by the arms. She could remember the way he looked into her eyes as he held onto her and steadied her.

Just his touch had made her heart skip a beat and every nerve in her body tingle with excitement. She was sure he had wanted to kiss her. She had no trouble remembering that she wanted him to.

She could also remember how she felt when he didn't kiss her and let go of her arms. It was a terrible feeling, one that was very hard for her to describe. Having him hold onto her had also frightened her a little, but she wasn't sure why. Was she afraid he would kiss her, or was she afraid that he wouldn't?

Lora glanced down at her cup of coffee to think about what had happened last night.

Every detail that she could remember caused her to realize he had done nothing wrong. They had coffee and crunch, walked outside to look at her new car, they had even had a conversation that had been pleasant, and boring, she thought. It seemed they had done nothing to try to find out if they were even compatible.

Just the thought of the word "compatible" caused Lora to cringe. It seemed so sterile, so unexciting. Of all the things in the world that Lora wanted, compatible didn't seem to be very important. However, love and loyalty were very important.

"Why can't I have a romantic and passionate love affair with a sexy man like Mark?" she asked herself. "Life should be fun and exciting."

Her thoughts turned to Kim and some of the things she had said to her. Lora knew Kim enjoyed life and what it had to offer. She could see no reason that she shouldn't do the same. She had seen Kim almost throw herself at Mark. As a result, he took her for a ride in the woods on horseback. Now that was romantic, or at least it could be given the right situation.

Lora knew from her conversation with Kim that they had spent most of the time talking about her. Kim had also told her if she had feelings for Mark and didn't go after him, she would. Lora had no doubt in her mind that Kim would go after Mark, if she didn't.

She turned and looked out the window toward the barn. It was at that moment she saw Mark walk out from behind a row of trees and head toward the barn. He took long strides and walked as if he had a purpose. She watched him for a moment, trying to decide what she should do.

"Kim was right," Lora said to herself.

With that thought in mind, she jumped up and headed for her bedroom to get dressed.

Once in her bedroom, she quickly decided to put on jeans and a blouse that would show off her figure. She would show Mark that she could fill out a pair of jeans and a blouse as well as any woman.

It was then that it occurred to her that she didn't have any tight fitting jeans with her and she wouldn't have any until the movers brought her things to her. Lora decided she would have to do the best she could with what she had and all she had was a pair of nicely tailored slacks and a flowered blouse. They looked good on her, but might not be as sexy as Mark might like.

She let out a brief sigh and started to dress. It wasn't long and she was ready to go out to the barn and talk to Mark. A quick look in the mirror let her know that the slacks she had did a good job of showing off her figure and did it with a little more class than jeans.

Mark was awake before the sun was up. It had been a long night of tossing and turning. He still wasn't sure about Lora. Last evening had been pleasant, but there had been moments when he wanted to do more than enjoy her coffee, Apple Crunch and talk about things like her new car, not that those things weren't important. He wanted to get to know her, to talk about themselves and share a little of themselves with each other.

The incident at her new car kept playing over and over in his mind. He had wanted to kiss her and let her know he cared a great deal for her, but her last boyfriend had made that difficult. He knew she might not be over him, and she might still have some reservations about the next man in her life. He could be patient if that's what it took.

His thoughts turned to Kim. She was a sexy little number and she had a bubbly personality, but Mark knew she was not his type. She was also Lora's best friend.

There was one more thing that came to mind. Since Lora had offered him the use of her barn, that allowed him to be on her property. It also made it possible for her to watch him and be around him without it seeming like she wanted him around. If that was the reason Lora had offered him the barn, there was a good chance it was Kim's idea. Kim was the one with the devious mind between the two of them.

Mark smiled at the thought that Kim might have gone to bat for him with Lora. He wasn't a hundred percent sure she had, but he couldn't think of any other reason for Lora to have changed her mind so abruptly. On the other hand, if it was Lora's idea, all the better for him.

It also crossed his mind that Lora might have offered him the use of the barn so he would be close by if Jeff decided to show up again. Mark rejected that as the reason; and even if it was so, he didn't really mind.

Mark got himself out of bed and dressed in work clothes. He had horses to take care. He went out to the kitchen and started fixing his breakfast. While it was cooking, he fed Casey. After he ate his breakfast, he was ready to get started on his routine chores.

As he stepped outside, he noticed the crew was already hard at work on the new barn. They had made pretty good progress on it. It crossed his mind that he hoped they didn't get it done too quickly.

"Mr. Howard," the foreman called to him.

Mark looked over at the foreman, then walked over to him. He looked at the foreman wondering what he wanted.

"Mr. Howard, do you know where your horses are?"

"Yes. Why?"

"Oh. We didn't see them in the pasture as we drove up. The last few days they would come running across the pasture and up to the fence when we came in. Today they aren't around. I was afraid one of my men might have left a gate open by mistake," the foreman explained.

"I'm sorry. I guess I should have told you. I started boarding them at my neighbor's last night. She offered me the use of her barn until mine is finished," he said with a grin.

"Oh," he said, his face showing his relief. "That wouldn't happen to be the nice looking woman with the wheelchair I saw when we first started working on your barn?"

"As a matter of fact, it is, but she doesn't need the wheelchair any more. She got her casts off and is doing very well."

"Good to hear it," he said.

"It looks like the barn is coming along."

"Yes, it is. We will be ready for the electrician in a couple of days."

"Good," Mark said, then turned and started off toward Lora's pasture.

As Mark rounded the row of trees that blocked off most of the view of his house from Lora's, he looked up at her ranch house. He wondered if she was up, yet. He thought about going up to the house to see if she would like to have coffee with him at his place, but he remembered she had said the movers were coming with her things today.

There was also the fact that he had chores to do in the barn.

Mark didn't want to impose on her any more than necessary. He had already decided it would be best if he took it slow with her. Mark was already imposing on her enough without trying to spend all his time with her. He was sure she had things to do, too.

By the time Mark got to the barn, Casey had finished his breakfast and had caught up with him. Mark started by taking the horses out of their stalls and leading them outside. Lora had offered him the use of her pasture, as well as the barn; so Mark let his horses loose in her pasture to graze.

Once the horses were out of the way, Mark returned to the barn. After gathering the necessary tools, he began mucking out the stalls. He loaded the muck into a wheelbarrow and wheeled it out to the back of the barn. Mark found a pile behind the barn that had apparently been there for years. It had weeds growing over it. He added what he had in the wheelbarrow to the pile. He thought it would be a good idea if he were to haul the pile out and spread it around in the pasture. It would make excellent fertilizer.

After he had finished mucking out the stalls, he realized that he didn't have any fresh straw to spread out in the stalls for bedding. He would have to go back to his place to get some.

He put all the tools away except for the pitchfork he would need to spread the straw around inside the stalls. He leaned the pitchfork up against one of the stalls and headed out the backdoor.

Mark was well on his way back to his storage shed for the straw when Lora entered the front of the barn. She could see him walking across the pasture toward his place from the back door of the barn. A feeling of disappointment came over her as she watched him walk away.

Lora looked around the barn and at the stalls. She wasn't sure how he did things, but if he was any kind of a rancher he was not finished with the stalls. He still had to put down fresh straw and spread it around inside the stalls.

Lora also noticed he had not put away all the tools. The pitchfork was still leaning against one of the stalls. That indicated to her he would be back before very long.

She was disappointed he had left, but she was feeling a little better with the thought he would be returning soon to finish his chores in the barn. Since she didn't have to be at her town house until eleven to meet the movers, she had time to wait for him to return.

Lora turned and looked around the barn. It had been a long time since she had been in the barn. The old barn brought back some very wonderful memories for her. She could remember playing in the barn with a couple of her cousins when she was barely a teenager.

It was then that she noticed the bales of hay neatly stacked in one of the stalls. She knew Mark had brought them over last evening to feed his horses. It reminded Lora of the years past when she would play with her cousins on the hay bales in the loft. She smiled as she remembered getting her very first kiss at the age of fourteen from her older cousin in this very barn. If she remembered, he was sixteen. It took place behind the stacks of hay in the loft. She had thought of that time often and how special it had been to her.

She slowly walked around inside the barn as she looked at everything there. Lora opened the tack bin and found her grandfather's old saddle. It was covered with dust and dirt, but otherwise looked to be in pretty good condition. Maybe a good cleaning with some saddle soap would make it useful again, she thought.

Along with a couple of old bridles and several old ropes, she found a pair of spurs. They were made of silver and had fancy decoration across the strap. She could remember her grandfather wearing them when he got all dressed up for a parade in Denver on the fourth of July when she was a little girl.

Lora was a little surprised at the memories the old barn brought to mind. She had forgotten how much the ranch had meant to her, especially after her father had walked out. Her grandfather had become the male figure in her life.

It was that thought that caused her to wonder about Mark. She wondered if he had had the chance to meet and get to know her grandfather.   Lora decided she would ask Mark when he returned.

She looked up in time to see Mark coming across the pasture in his truck. She could see he had it loaded with bales of straw. She smiled as she waited and watched him drive up next to the barn door.

Mark saw Lora standing in the door of the barn. He smiled at the sight of her waiting for him, at least that is what it looked like. She was wearing a pair of slacks that fit her well. It was the first time he had seen her dressed in nicely tailored slacks. All he could think about was that she was a fine looking woman.

He pulled to a stop just outside the barn and stepped out of his truck. As he walked toward her, he looked her over. The slacks accented her narrow waist and the smooth flare of her hips. The flowered blouse did nothing to hide the fact she was every bit a woman and all in proportion for her overall build. Mark couldn't help but think she was one very nice looking woman. He even liked the way she had done her hair.

"I've got to say you are dressed a little too nice for mucking out stalls," he said with a smile.

Lora found his smile to be captivating and the way he looked at her was intoxicating. It made her feel as though he thought of her as maybe even a bit sexy although he had not come out and said so. His comment also showed he had a sense of humor.

"Thank you. I figured if I dressed nice enough you wouldn't ask me to help," she said playfully as she smiled back at him and tipped her head to one side.

"I think you figured about right. I guess I'll have to ask for your help some other time."

Lora was glad when he turned his back to her and started walking back to his truck. The way he looked at her made her feel a little uncomfortable, but it was an uncomfortable feeling she sort of liked, maybe a little too much.

"Are you going somewhere?" he asked as he lugged the first bale of straw off the back of the truck and started toward one of the stalls with it.

"As a matter of fact, yes. But I don't have to go right way."

"Must be some pretty fancy place for you to be all dressed up. You look very nice," he said without looking at her.

Mark was almost afraid to look at her. As far as he was concerned she was stunning and he liked what he saw. She could distract him easily dressed like that.

"No, actually it's not. I have to go into town to meet the movers. They are going to be at my town house at eleven o'clock. I have to tell them what to pack and bring here," she explained.

"Pretty nice outfit for that kind of work," he said as he glanced over his shoulder to take another quick look at her.

"I have to confess. I wouldn't normally dress this way except that most of my clothes are still at my town house."

"Oh?"

"Yes. I didn't really have a need for them until now. I've spent most of my time since the accident in sweat pants and a robe. I'd have never been able to get my jeans or my sweatshirts over my casts."

"I, for one, am glad that you don't need the casts any more," he said without turning around.

Lora wasn't sure how she should take his comment since she could not see his face. But when added to what else he had said before, she was sure he meant it in only the nicest of ways. It pleased her a great deal to know he found her pretty.

Lora watched him as he cut the twine on the bales of straw and began spreading the straw inside the stall. As he reached around the stall from the inside to get the pitchfork, he looked at her and smiled.

"This could get a little dusty and dirty when I pitchfork the straw around in the stall. You might want to wait outside until I'm done," he suggested as he took a quick look at her again.

"That's probably a good idea. I'll have some iced tea for you on the patio when you're done, if you like."

"That would be nice," he said with a smile.

Mark leaned against the pitchfork while he watched Lora leave the barn. He was still leaning on it when she was well outside the barn. It was not easy for him to take his eyes off her. He couldn't help but watch the gentle sway of her shapely hips as she walked toward the house.

"Damn, she's beautiful," Mark said to himself under his breath.

He shook his head and then returned to his work. When he finished spreading the straw around in the stalls, he put some hay in the trough for when he brought the horses in to bed them down for the night. Then he put the pitchfork away and looked around. Everything was done for now.

CHAPTER NINETEEN

Mark looked out the front door of the barn toward the house. He was feeling rather dirty and questioned if he should go up to the house. It occurred to him that Lora was not like Barbara. She would understand that Mark would be dirty after working in the barn. Lora was at least part country girl and understood what it took to care for horses.

He took his hat off and slapped it against his jeans in an effort to get as much of the dust and dirt off his pants as he could. He put his hat back on and used his hands to brush as much of the dust off the front of his shirt as he could before leaving the barn.

As Mark walked toward the house, he could see Lora come out of the house with a tray in her hands. She set it down on the table on the patio.

"Are you done?" she asked as she smiled at him.

"Until tonight," he said as he walked up the steps to the patio.

"Here you go. I figure you could use this," she said as she handed him a tall glass full of iced tea.

"Thank you," he replied as he took it from her small hand.

"Sit down, please."

Mark sat down on one of the patio chairs. He was feeling a little uncomfortable since he was so dirty and she looked so dressed up.

"I've wanted to ask you something," she said.

"Shoot. What's on your mind?" he asked then took a long drink of iced tea.

"Did you know my grandfather?"

"Yes. Yes I did. He was a very interesting man."

"Did you like him?"

"Sure. I don't know if you knew this, but he would go riding with me, sometimes as often as three times a week. There was nothing he liked better than getting on a horse and riding on the U.S. Forest Service land. He was a good man. I liked spending time with him. He even helped with my horses from time to time. I think he missed not having some of his own."

"I hadn't seen him for several years before he died. I've always been sorry about that," she said, her voice taking on a sad tone.

"He talked about you, although I didn't know it was you at the time."

"He did?" she asked with a smile.

"Oh yes. He liked you. He said you were a bright spot in his life."

Mark noticed Lora had a sad look on her face. He hoped he had not said too much to upset her, but he couldn't lie to her.

Lora looked up at Mark and smiled even though she had tears in her eyes.

"I liked him, too. I only wish I had spent more time with him when he got older and couldn't get around much any more."

"You shouldn't beat yourself up over it. He knew you thought a great deal of him. He talked about you and how busy your life was. He was glad you could come see him as often as you did. Do you know you're the only grandchild that ever came to see him after he could no longer get around?" Mark asked softly.

"I didn't know that," she replied as tears ran down her cheeks.

"He said he wished you would have come up here and lived with him. But he also said he understood that a beautiful young woman like you might prefer the city life to living up here with an old man."

"Did he really say that?" she asked not really believing what Mark had said, but hoping it was true.

"Yes, he did," Mark assured her.

Lora turned and looked off across the pasture and sipped on her iced tea. She wasn't really paying any attention to the pasture, she was thinking about her grandfather and how much she missed him.

Mark sipped on the tea and watched her. He hoped he had not caused her too much sorrow talking about her grandfather, but she had asked. Mark also felt she would want to know that her grandfather had loved her.

"What time do you have to meet the movers?" Mark asked, hoping that changing the subject would help her.

He didn't want to disturb her thoughts, but he didn't want her to be late, either. She turned around and looked at him then looked at her watch.

"I have to meet them at eleven. I've got a little while yet before I have to leave," she said.

Lora took another sip of her tea as she looked at Mark. She found she liked being around him. It didn't hurt any that he had liked her grandfather. That thought gave her an idea.

"How would you like to come with me into town?"

"I'm in no condition to go into town," he said with a chuckle.

"You have time to clean up. Besides, I think you asked me to lunch awhile back, but we didn't go," she said as she smiled at him.

"I guess you're right."

"Then you'll go into town with me?"

"Sure. You'll have to give me time to shower," he said as he set the tea on the table and stood up.

"You don't think I'm going to take you in my new car looking like that, do you?"

"I would hope not. I'll be back shortly."

"I'll pick you up in about twenty-five minutes at your door?" she asked.

"Twenty-five minutes? I can do it in twenty-five minutes."

Mark turned and walked off the patio and down toward the barn. He jumped into his truck and took off for home.

Lora watched him as he drove across the pasture and around the corner behind the row of trees. She smiled to herself. It was the first time she had felt like going somewhere with a man in some time.

As soon as he was out of sight, Lora picked up the glasses and put them on the tray. She then picked up the tray and looked off toward Mark's place before she turned and carried it into the house.

After putting things away and putting the glasses in the dishwasher, she went into her bedroom. She ran a comb through her hair and made sure her lipstick was on good. After making sure the house was locked up and she had everything she needed, she picked up her purse and walked out the front door to her car. She then drove to Mark's place by the road.

Mark drove his truck around to the front of the house and jumped out of it. He ran inside and began undressing as soon as he was in the house. It didn't take him long to shower and shave, and to get dressed in a nice pair of kaki slacks and a red polo shirt. What he had decided to wear would make him almost as dressy as Lora and it would be acceptable at any fine restaurant for the noon meal. He had no idea where they would be going for lunch, but he was ready for almost any place she might suggest.

As he stepped out of the house, he saw Lora coming down the driveway in her new Durango. His timing had been perfect. He waited for her to pull up in front of the house and stop. Mark reached over, opened the door and got in.

"Right on time," he said.

"I don't think I've ever met a man who cleaned up so well in such a short time," Lora said with a smile.

"Thank you, I think," he replied with a chuckle.

"I'm sorry. That didn't sound very nice, did it?"

"It's fine. I knew what you meant."

"Say, would you like to drive my new car?"

"No. I'll drive it some other time. Besides, I don't know where your town house is. It would be easier if you drive," Mark said as he reached around and grabbed the seatbelt.

"Okay," she said as she watched him buckle up.

Lora wasn't sure what to think. This was a guy that didn't care if she drove. It seemed all the other men that she had ever gone out with insisted on driving.

Lora put the car in gear and drove out onto the road. It wasn't long and they were cruising down the interstate toward Denver. She pulled off the interstate on the outskirts of Lakewood, then turned into a nice housing area that was made up of some very nice town houses.

"Is this where you live?" Mark asked.

"Not after today. I gave them notice I was moving. I still have the place until the end of the month, but I can't see any reason to be paying utilities on two places or rent on one when the other one is free and clear."

"That makes sense," Mark agreed as she turned into a drive in front of a one-car garage.

Mark looked up at the town house. It was a very nice looking place, but it looked as if they were all stuffed together like sardines. He much preferred the more open space of his mountain ranch.

"Damn," Lora said almost too softly for Mark to hear, but he did hear her.

"What's the matter?" Mark asked as he quickly turned toward her to see what the problem was.

"That's Jeff's car coming down the street."

"Are you sure?"

"Yes," she replied as she let out a long sigh.

Mark watched the car as it pulled up in front of the town house. He wondered what Jeff was doing there. There was no doubt Lora had made it clear she didn't want to see him again.

"Please don't start anything," Lora said as she turned and looked at Mark.

"I promise I will not start anything, but I will not put up with anything from him," Mark said looking directly into Lora's eyes.

Lora didn't know what to say. She turned, opened the door and stepped out of her car. She heard the door on the other side of the car shut and knew Mark had gotten out.

Lora stood and watched as Jeff got out of his car and started up the driveway toward her. He looked like he was mad. She knew he was probably upset over the fact Mark was with her. She got the impression he had expected her to be alone.

"What's he doing here?" Jeff asked, his voice showing his displeasure.

"That's none of your business. What are you doing here?" Lora asked, obviously not pleased to see him.

"I knew you got your casts off. I thought you would be returning here so you could get back to work. I figured we could talk and get this whole mess straightened out," he said trying to ignore Mark.

"There is nothing to straighten out. I told you before I didn't want to see you again and that it was over between us."

"You don't mean that. Besides, she doesn't mean anything to me," he said as a way to excuse his infidelity.

"Then I must not mean anything to you either. If I did, you would not be messing around with another woman."

"But honey, it was just ah, ah, a fling."

"You and your fling hurt me. I can forgive you for just about anything, but that. I don't want to see you again or hear from you again. If I have to, I will call the police and have you arrested for harassing me," Lora said, then turned around to walk away.

Just then Jeff made a big mistake. He reached out and grabbed Lora by the arm.

Mark had made it a point to stay out of it until Jeff grabbed her. He was not about to let him manhandle her.

"Take your hands off her," Mark said as he stepped forward.

Jeff just looked at Mark for a second before he let go of Lora.

"You think you're pretty tough. Well, I don't think you are. I think it's about time I whip your ass," Jeff said angrily.

"Jeff, you get out of here before I call the police," Lora said.

Mark made no move toward Jeff, nor did he back away. He didn't even respond to Jeff's challenge. Jeff had done what he had told him to do and that was to let go of Lora. Mark was not going to throw the first punch, and he was not going to start a fight with Jeff. This was all going to be Jeff's doing, and whatever Mark did was going to be in self-defense or to protect Lora.

"I think you should get in your car and leave before you get in any deeper than you already are," Mark said calmly.

"I'm not the one who's in over his head," Jeff said with a stupid grin.

"I believe you are in over your head. If you have brains enough to think past the end of your nose, you will see you're not going to get out of this with anything but a lot of trouble," Mark said.

"And just how do you figure that, cowboy?" once again putting the emphasis on the word cowboy.

"Simple. If you and I get into a fight here on the street, there are going to be several witnesses that will testify that you started it by throwing the first punch. Take a look around and you will see there are several people watching us."

Mark waited while Jeff looked around. There were two people right across the street watching them. There was another one next door who could easily hear what was going on as well as see it.

Mark could see the change in Jeff's expression. He also knew he now had Jeff's undivided attention.

"If you are stupid enough to throw the first punch, I will first of all beat the hell out of you, and then I will call the police and have you arrested for attempted assault. I really believe your law firm would not be very happy to see it reported in the paper. Don't you agree?" Mark asked, keeping his voice calm.

Mark just stood there between Jeff and Lora and waited for a response from Jeff. He didn't notice Lora had stepped up next to him until she reached out and took hold of his arm.

"I want you to stay away from me. Since you have shown me you are unwilling to leave me alone, you give me no choice but to go to the courthouse tomorrow and request a restraining order to keep you away from me," Lora said flatly.

Jeff turned a little pale over her statement. He had to know that newspaper reporters made it a practice of going to the courthouse on a daily basis looking for things they considered news. If they found his name on a restraining order, they might just start investigating the reason such an order was issued. That would not go over very well with his father or the other partners of the law firm.

"That won't be necessary. I will not bother you again. You will one day be sorry you didn't see things differently because I will not forgive you and take you back," Jeff said.

Lora and Mark just stood there and watched him as he turned and stomped back to his car. As soon as Jeff got into his car and drove off, Lora looked up at Mark.

"I'm sorry," she said.

"It's okay," Mark said as he reached out and put his hand over her arm.

Jeff had no more than disappeared around the corner when the small moving van pulled up in front of the town house. Lora and Mark were still standing in the driveway. She was still holding onto his arm, and he still had his hand on her arm. Lora let go of Mark's arm when the three men got out of the van and walked toward them.

"Are you Lora Winters?" the oldest of the three men asked.

"Yes."

"Well, if you'll show us what you want packed, we'll get started.

"Right this way," she said as she turned and started toward the town house.

For the next hour or so, Mark stayed out of the way. He watched as Lora gave instructions to the movers, and the older man got the rest of the crew started on packing.

One thing Mark noticed about the town house was it was a little larger than he had expected. It was a very nice home and he could see Lora living in such a place. The strange thing to him was he could also see her living at the small mountain ranch house. The more he got to know about her, the more he liked her.

"I think we can go to lunch now," Lora said disturbing Mark's thoughts.

"You don't need to hang around?"

"No. They can do this without us here. We can go get something to eat and come back," she suggested.

"Okay," Mark agreed. "Where would you like to go?"

"I don't know. Why don't you pick a place?"

Mark smiled as he took hold of her hand and started out the door. They walked hand in hand to her car. When they got to her car, she handed him the keys and smiled.

"Since you know where we're going, you drive."

Mark smiled at her, then opened the door. He waited for Lora to get in. Once she was in, he went around and got in behind the wheel.

"Are you really hungry?"

"Yes, I'm famished. I didn't have much of a breakfast."

"Okay. I know a great place to eat. I hope you like beef?"

"I like beef," she replied with a smile.

Mark turned the key and started the car. He backed out of the driveway and headed for downtown Denver.

"Where are we going?"

"Have you ever been to The Keg Steakhouse and Bar?"

"No. Is it good?"

"Excellent."

Lora and Mark had an excellent steak dinner. During dinner they had a chance to talk. Lora explained what had happened the night of the accident. Mark was patient and listened to her.

When she was finished, he told her about Barbara, their breakup, and the fact that she had his barn burned to the ground. It became a time of growing close as they each let the other know a little more about themselves.

When they returned to her town house, they found that most of her things had been packed. The moving crew was beginning to load the truck.

In order to stay out of the way, Lora and Mark stood leaning against Lora's car. Mark had his arm around her shoulder and Lora was nestled up against Mark's side. They continued to talk about the things they liked and the things they didn't like. It soon became apparent they had many things in common.

"When are they going to deliver your things?"

"I don't know."

"It might be a good idea if we find out?"

"Okay,"

Mark took his arm from around Lora's shoulder. Together they walked into her town house to talk to the older member of the crew. He said they could deliver it late this afternoon or the first thing tomorrow morning. Lora decided it would be best if they delivered this afternoon as she had little to wear at the ranch.

Once the moving van was loaded and had left, Lora took a quick walk through the town house to make sure everything had been taken that belonged to her. Then with Mark behind the wheel, they drove back to the ranch. On the way up, they passed the moving van on a long steep hill leading into the foothills. They beat the moving van to her ranch by close to twenty minutes.

Since there was nothing for Mark to do, he decided he would take care of his horses while Lora directed the movers to put things in the rooms she wanted them in. When they were done unloading the moving van, she paid the driver and thanked him and his crew.

CHAPTER TWENTY

AS SOON AS THE MOVERS were gone, Lora stood in the middle of the living room and looked at all the boxes that were stacked here and there. She knew the other rooms were as disorganized as the living room. She also knew that once she started unpacking, it would be more of a mess before it would get better. At the moment it looked like an impossible task.

Lora was beginning to feel a bit tired. Her ankle was hurting a little. She remembered what her doctor had told her. There was no doubt she should get off her feet, but there was so much to do. She sat down and leaned over to rub her ankle. She was rubbing it when Mark came in the door.

"Your ankle hurting?"

She looked up at him and smiled, but it was clear she was in some pain. It was also clear that Mark was concerned.

"Yeah. A little."

Mark walked over and sat down beside her on the sofa. She leaned against him as she looked up at him. He leaned down and kissed her gently on the lips. There was little passion behind the kiss. It was almost as if he was testing to see if she would object to him kissing her.

Since she didn't seem to object, he kissed her again. This time the kiss had a little more passion in it. It was still a light kiss, but one intended to let her know he cared a great deal about her.

Mark's second kiss sent a spark of desire through her entire body. It surprised her, but she decided she would not resist.

When the second kiss was over, she leaned back and looked into Mark's eyes for a moment. She then leaned closer to him and let him kiss her again. Only this time, she put more of herself into it. It wasn't long before it had turned into a deep passionate kiss. It left both of them wanting more.

When they finally broke off the kiss, they were both breathing hard. Lora had never felt a kiss like that before. It had consumed her whole body. Her entire being told her to grab on to him and not let go of him.

Mark just looked at the woman beside him. He had never had a kiss like it before, either. He had already given into the fact he was in love with Lora, and it was something very special. It told him that she was in love with him.

"Maybe, I should go and let you go to bed. I think it might be best if you got some rest, don't you?"

"Yes, but have you looked at my bedroom. I don't think I can even find my bed," she replied softly.

He looked into her eyes. Up to now he had been very careful about what he said and what he suggested. But there was something in her eyes that told him that he could stick his neck out a little without serious repercussions if he did it right. That would mean there should be no demands on her that she couldn't refuse comfortably.

"What would you think about coming over to my place and sleeping in my bed?" he asked, almost immediately wishing he hadn't suggested it.

She looked at him for what seemed like a very long time. He was afraid she might think that he was moving too fast.

"Ah - - just one thing I would like to know."

"Sure."

"Will we be able to wake up and watch the sun come up from your bed?"

"That depends."

"On what?"

"On if we wake up early enough," Mark said with a smile.

"Okay," she replied as she leaned over and kissed him again.

"Is there anything you would like to take with you?"

"Like what?"

"A nightgown, maybe?"

"Do I need one?"

"Not for me," he said with a grin.

"I'm ready, then."

It was only a matter of a few minutes before Mark was helping Lora to her car. He locked up her house for her and drove her to his house. Mark parked her car out in front beside his truck.

Since her ankle was hurting her a little, he carried her into his ranch house and into the bedroom. He put her down on the edge of his bed and stepped back.

"I need a shower after taking care of the horses. Can you get ready for bed without any help?"

"I think so. My ankle doesn't hurt that much."

Mark started to turn and leave the room, but was stopped by Lora.

"Mark, do I get a kiss before you go," she asked looking up at him.

Mark smiled and returned to the side of the bed. He leaned down, put his hand under her chin and tipped her face up to him. He leaned forward until his lips met hers. He kissed her, then leaned back and smiled at her.

"Will that hold you until I get back?"

"If you don't take too long," she said with a smile.

"I'll be back in a couple of minutes."

Mark turned around and went into the bathroom. When he returned, he found Lora under the sheet with her eyes closed. He noticed her clothes were neatly laid over a nearby chair.

When he turned back to look at her in the bed, he could see the outline of her slender body under the sheet. As he stepped up along side the bed, Lora opened her eyes. She lifted up the sheet for him to climb in with her.

Mark slipped into the bed. He leaned over and turned off the bedside light. There was a slight glow from the yard light out back. He scooted down in the bed and then laid down next to her.

Lora rolled over against his side. He could feel the warmth of her naked body against him. He wrapped her in his arms and leaned over and kissed her.

Lora liked the feel of Mark against her body, but most of all she liked the feel of his arms around her. She was not sure it was a good idea to spend the night with him, but she had never wanted anything more in her whole life. She wanted this to be the first of many nights with him.

As their passion for each other grew, Mark rolled Lora up over him. She stretched her naked body out over top of him as they kissed. She had never felt more wanted than she did at the moment. The feel of Mark's hands exploring her body sent waves of desire over her skin.

The feel of Lora's soft smooth skin under his hands and the feel of her firm breasts pressing against his chest sent Mark's need for her to the sky. He needed her as well as wanted her.

"I love you," he whispered between kisses.

"I love you, too. Make love to me," she whispered.

Mark rolled her over on her back. Taking their time and enjoying each other, they made love. It was late when they finally fell asleep in each other's arms.

When morning came, Lora woke up to find herself securely wrapped in Mark's arms. He had one arm under her head and the other over her. He had one of her firm breasts cupped gently in his hand. It felt good the way he held her. She could also feel his warm breath on the back of her neck.

She looked out the patio doors at the sun as it was coming up over the horizon. The colors in the sky were beautiful. The fact she was in the arms of the man she loved only helped make the morning something special.

She reached over and put her hand over Mark's hand on her breast and pressed it to her. She liked the feel of his hand on her.

"You better be careful or you will be in this bed for a very long time."

"Are you referring to today, or to a somewhat longer period of time?" she asked, wondering what he was going to say.

"Oh, for a very long time."

"I like that idea," she said as she turned over in his arms.

She rolled up against him and kissed him. He returned her kiss with as much passion as she had shown him.

"You're missing the sunrise," he said as he looked into her eyes.

"I'm sure there will be more," she replied as she scooted up against him and kissed him hard.